Long-Lost Sister

ALSO BY N.L. HINKENS

The Caregiver
The Neighbor
Long-Lost Sister

LONG LOST SISTER

N.L. HINKENS

JOFFE BOOKS

Joffe Books, London
www.joffebooks.com

First published in Great Britain in 2025

© N.L. Hinkens

Cover art by Nick Castle

ISBN: 978-1-80573-209-9

CHAPTER 1

I have a sister. A *sister*.

The word rumbles around inside my head like a lone tennis shoe in a dryer. Jarring. Misplaced. Offbeat.

If it hadn't been for the myancestry.com membership my best friend Marco gifted me for my birthday, I would never even have known my sister existed. Marco knew I was mildly curious about my roots, but too cheap, and possibly chicken, to investigate them. The only thing I know about my biological family is that my mother was sixteen when I was born, and she died a few years later. My birth certificate lists my father as *unknown*. Seems unlikely, but I guess that's how my mother wanted it.

I start to log in to Facebook to indulge my curiosity about the sister I didn't know I had, when I notice the time. I can't be late for group. It's the one commitment I never waver on. I'm not proud of the turn my life took a decade ago, but I'm heading in the right direction now, and I don't want to mess things up again. I still have flashbacks to the mistake that kick-started my free fall into delinquency. "Mistake" is the wrong word, but it slips off the tongue easily, lending me grace I don't deserve. I hate the term "flashback" too. It's inadequate — underplaying what happened that day as a blip in time. The truth is, it's a soul-destroying movie that plays on repeat in my brain, dragging me back through the years to a place I don't want to go. But I can never rid myself of the memory because what I did that day is engraved for all to see in the life I destroyed.

Snatching up my purse, I hurry out to my 1999 Camry and jam the key in the ignition. I'm rewarded with a rapid clicking sound that makes my heart plummet. I try turning the engine over several more times before admitting defeat. The battery has been on the blink for the past few days, but I can't afford a new one. My landlord just raised the rent, and I need to find a new place to live pronto, or I'll be sleeping in my car. I've already picked up an extra shift at the Wicked Scone just to make ends meet. I slam the steering wheel in frustration before fishing my phone from my purse to call Marco.

"Hey, Piper. What's up?"

"I'm not going to make it tonight. I'm sitting in my car right now, all ready to go, but my battery's dead."

"Want me to pick you up?" he asks. "I assume that's why you're calling."

I scrunch my eyes shut, trying not to feel defensive at his blunt delivery. I know he doesn't mean to come across that way. He's not one for fluff and feelings; his brain is wired for practicality and problem-solving — for which I'm grateful. He's bailed me out many times before.

"No, that's all right," I reply, yanking the key back out. "By the time you drive to my place and back, we'd miss half the meeting. No sense both of us losing out. I'm just bummed because I have some exciting news."

"Really? What?"

"It's too important to tell you over the phone. Come round afterward and I'll fill you in."

Marco groans. "Seriously? You're going to keep me in suspense 'til then? I'm tempted to skip and come right over."

"We both know that's not a good idea."

"Right. See you around nine."

I hang up and trudge back into my apartment. This sucks. I have no idea how I'm going to get to work in the morning. I could take my bike, but it's older than my Camry and it would take me the best part of an hour in the rush-hour traffic. I'm not even sure the tires will stay inflated long enough to get me there.

I pour myself a glass of water, reach for my laptop, and plonk down on the couch. Maybe a night in was meant to be. After all, what could be more important than tracking down my younger sister — I'm guessing she's younger — and making a connection? I type the name *Callie Madden* into the Facebook search field, hoping she has the same last name that's on my birth certificate. My palms are already sweating as I scroll through the list of names and click on any that look promising. I'm trying not to get my hopes up. It's hard to tell from a thumbnail if any of the women look like me.

When I've exhausted the list of exact matches, I start going through spelling variations. That's when I stumble on a profile that stops me in my tracks: *Callie Madden-Bramston*. I click on it and stare at the stunning cover photo of a bride standing on the balcony of some ritzy resort hotel in the Bahamas — according to the caption. My heart jolts in my chest. Something about her resonates with me. She looks familiar.

I begin frantically scrolling through the rest of the photos in her feed until I come to a close-up of her and an extremely good-looking man who I assume is her husband. Two flawless, model lookalikes leaning their heads together, grinning at the camera. I examine each of Callie's features in turn. The similarities are undeniable, although she looks a few years younger than me. She has my eyes and lips — thinner on top with a full pout on the bottom. Her hair is the same rich chestnut color as mine, but hers is expertly highlighted and curled.

Sinking back against the ratty pillows on the couch, I take a few shallow breaths to calm my thudding heart. It's her. I'm sure it's my sister. But now that I've found her, I'm not experiencing the euphoric emotions I thought I would. She looks

3

happy — like she has her life together and is married to the man of her dreams. If the smile on her face is any indication, she has everything she wants in life already.

I slam the lid of my laptop closed. I can't message her. She wouldn't want anything to do with me — especially if she knew what I'd done.

CHAPTER 2

It's nine forty-five by the time Marco finally shows up.

"You're late," I chide, ushering him into my apartment —
all 400 square feet of cracked linoleum and sagging wallpaper.

He sinks down in my rickety thrift-store chair, sniffing tentatively at the faint smell of mildew that pervades the
space, and runs a hand over the back of his thinning hair. He's
only thirty-two but baldness is clearly in his near future. He's
self-conscious about it, so I tell him all the time he's going
to rock the nerd look. His perfect tan and striking blue eyes
compensate for the receding hairline.

"A couple of new people showed up tonight and we ran
a little over," he explains. "This one woman felt compelled to
share her entire life story by way of introduction. Terry fell
asleep halfway through and started snoring. I had to elbow
him in the ribs to get him to straighten up and pay attention."

I let out a snort as I open the refrigerator and frown at the
contents. "What do you want to drink?"

"What do you have?"

"Nothing," I say, slamming the door shut. I've been
avoiding making a grocery run. The price of everything gives
me heart palpitations. "How about a cup of tea?"

5

"Works for me," Marco replies. "While you're brewing it, I'm going to change out your car battery. I picked up a new one at Walmart on my way over."

I give an abashed grin. Marco works in cyber security and makes a ton more money than me, but I hate feeling like I'm taking advantage of him. "I can't afford to pay you back until my next check, and even that's a stretch."

He waves a hand dismissively. "This one's on me. It's a trade for all the spaghetti you've cooked for me."

He hightails it out of the kitchen before I can protest. A few measly boxes of pasta hardly compensate for a new car battery. As I reach for the kettle, a sense of relief floods me. At least I can sleep soundly tonight knowing I won't have to hitch a ride to work. That's one problem solved. But I'm still only a hairsbreadth away from financial disaster.

My thoughts turn to my supposed sister's Facebook feed. Callie Madden-Bramston doesn't look like she knows what it means to be hanging on by her fingernails — worrying about how to scrounge up enough to pay rent and utilities. It remains to be seen whether she'll be sympathetic to my plight or turn up her dermaplaned nose at me.

Marco returns from the garage a few minutes later, and I hand him a mug of tea. "Thanks again. You saved me a sleepless night. I had no idea how I was going to get to work in the morning."

"You could have called me." He plasters on a lopsided grin as he sits down at the kitchen table, tea in hand. "But you'd never ask, would you?"

I shrug and pull out the chair next to him. "I feel bad. You're always rescuing me."

He blows on his tea and takes a sip, peering thoughtfully over the rim at me. "Works both ways. I'd have fallen off the wagon a bunch of times by now if it hadn't been for you talking sense into me."

He hefts an eyebrow. "So, what's this burning secret you wanted to tell me about in person?"

I fetch my laptop and set it up on the table between us. Clicking on Callie's Facebook page, I pull up the photo I found earlier. "Recognize this woman?" I ask, tapping a fingernail on the screen.

Marco scrunches his face up as he studies it. "Should I?"

"Doesn't she look *at all* familiar?" I say, blinking at him while pouting my lips in an exaggerated fashion.

His eyes bounce to and fro from the photo to my face. "Is she . . . a relative of yours?"

"She's my biological sister. I didn't even know I had one until I sent in my DNA to that site. She lives here in LA."

"Are you serious?" Marco reaches for the laptop and pulls it closer to peer more intently at the photo. "What about your father — did you find him too?"

I shake my head. "Either he hasn't taken the DNA test, or he's deceased. My sister's the only match that showed up."

"That's fantastic news." Marco darts a hesitant glance my way. "Isn't it? I mean, this is what you were hoping to find, a blood relative."

I let out a heavy sigh. "Yes, but I'm not so sure I want to make contact."

Marco frowns in confusion. "Why not?"

I take a long draft of tea before responding. "What if I'm an embarrassment to her?" I gesture at the screen. "Look at her! She's drop-dead gorgeous, her and her husband. They're living the high life — vacations, cars, exotic wedding with a designer dress. Why would she want me in her life?"

Marco sets his lips in a thin, disapproving line. "Quit beating yourself up. You haven't even given her an opportunity to get to know you yet. Why would you assume your sister is shallow enough to care more about money than she does about finding out she has a sibling?"

I scrub my hands over my face. "It's not just the money. How am I supposed to explain the mess I've made of things? Not everyone would welcome that kind of relative into their life."

Marco slurps his tea. "Give her a chance. She might not be as unwelcoming as you're pegging her to be. Besides, you don't have to confess your history of drunken stupors right out of the gate."

"Pretending I'm something I'm not. Great way to start a relationship." I bite my lip, locking eyes with Marco. "I've never come clean at group about why I started drinking in the first place. There's a lot you don't know about me either."

Marco squirms in his seat. "Whatever you did in the past, it's not going to affect our friendship."

I nod slowly, my pulse drumming in my ears. It's time to put that to the test. If he can't handle the truth, how can I expect my sister to do so?

And so, I tell him everything — almost everything.

CHAPTER 3

Marco doesn't say much after my shocking confession. Instead, he takes me in his arms and hugs me. He's the one true friend I've had since Emma died. He's had his fair share of grief himself, and he knows what it does to a person. It was heart-wrenching to learn at my first AA meeting that his young wife and baby daughter were murdered in a home invasion robbery. He drank away the pain, but now he's found a healthier way to deal with it.

"I still think you need to reach out to your sister," he says, when he releases me. "She deserves to know you exist. Once you've gotten to know her, you can decide how much of your life you can trust her with. It doesn't have to be a bare-your-soul relationship."

I know he's right, but it's still over a week later before I finally pluck up the courage to message Callie on Facebook. I'm on pins and needles for the next forty-eight hours before a response finally comes through.

Who is this? I don't have a sister.

9

My fingers shake as I tap out a reply.

I was adopted at birth. I found you on myancestry.com. I can show you the information I received. Can we meet? I live in the LA area too. I'm sure once you see me, you'll know I'm your sister. We look alike.

Callie makes me wait another whole day before messaging me back.

Meet me at Starbucks in the Waterfront Mall at noon tomorrow.

I reread the message out loud to make sure my eyes aren't imagining what I'm wanting to see. My stomach swirls with a mixture of dread and excitement. I'm going to have to take off early for lunch, but I can probably swing it with all the overtime I've been putting in lately.

I call Marco to tell him the good news. "She's agreed to meet me."

"I knew she would! I'm pumped — for both of you."

"I can't stop shaking every time I think about it. She looks so glamorous."

"Just be yourself. You got this!"

"Thanks for the pep talk, Marco. I'll let you know how it goes."

I hang up and reread Callie's message for the umpteenth time to make sure I've got the details right. I can't help being intimidated at the prospect of meeting her in person. She's impeccably dressed in every photo — manicured and pedicured to the hilt. My stomach drops when I think of my meager wardrobe. What on earth am I going to wear? I'll have to bring something with me to the bakery to change into. I can't show up in the faded T-shirt and jeans I usually wear to work. I spend the next hour trying on and discarding the pitiful collection of clothes in my closet. It's not like I can hope to match Callie's designer wardrobe, but I don't want to look

10

like a total slob the first time she sets eyes on me. I settle on a simple floral dress with boots and a cargo jacket. It may not be expensive, but it looks stylish in a bohemian sort of way. Before I can second-guess my choice, I pack the outfit in a bag and leave it in the car so I don't forget it.

* * *

When my alarm goes off the following morning, I jolt upright. *Callie!* Today's the day I get to meet my sister. I bolt out of bed, suddenly wide awake. Thirty minutes later, I'm showered and on my way to the Wicked Scone. I've already cleared it with my boss, Jenna, to take an early lunch but I haven't told her why. I'll see how things go with Callie first.

This could be another mistake I'll live to regret.

11

CHAPTER 4

"Morning Piper!" Jenna greets me with a cheerful grin as I come through the back door of the bakery. She drags a tray of cupcakes out of the oven and sets it aside to cool before fanning her face with her hands. "I made a few extra batches — we almost ran out last Friday."

I reach for my apron and tie it around my waist. "I'll take over here. You can get started on another mix."

She gives a grateful nod and heads over to the commercial stand mixer, leaving me in charge of getting the next batch into the ovens.

The minute we open the bakery doors, the weekend rush begins. I glance at the clock intermittently to make sure I don't run late for my lunch date. At 11:45 a.m. I undo my apron and let Jenna know I'm leaving.

"Everything all right?" she asks, a concerned note in her voice.

I should have known she'd pick up on my unease. She fusses over me like a mother hen.

"Yes. Fine, thanks. Just didn't sleep well last night. Got a crick in my neck." I roll my head around and wince, hoping my dramatic posturing looks halfway convincing. I hate lying

12

to Jenna — she's been so understanding of my struggles and encouraging of the strides I've made in the right direction.

Before she can engage me any further, I slip into the cramped bathroom to change and freshen up. Knowing my luck, Callie will come straight from the beauty salon glowing from a deep-tissue massage and an oxygen facial.

I hurry out to my car, grateful for my new battery. I need to figure out something to do for Marco in return. I could offer to cook him another meal, but these days it's a stretch to include pasta in my budget. I buckle my seatbelt and set an alarm on my phone for 1:00 p.m. I don't want to leave Jenna flying solo for too long.

It's normally only a five-minute drive to the mall but a slow-moving delivery truck ahead of me makes it much longer. I peel into a parking spot near the main entrance and dash inside. I'm six minutes late and sweating profusely from a turbo dose of nerves and exertion. What if Callie has already left? *Don't be ridiculous!* I'm being paranoid. No one would leave after only a few minutes of waiting to meet a newly discovered sibling.

By the time I arrive at the Starbucks near the food court on the second level of the mall, my chest is heaving from my sprint from the car. I glance around anxiously searching for Callie, but there's no sign of her anywhere. I slide into an unoccupied table and glance around once more to make sure I haven't missed her. Waves of illogical thoughts pound my brain. *She's ghosted me. She never had any intention of coming. She doesn't want anything to do with me.* My gaze flicks from store front to store front. Maybe she's waiting by one of the windows — sizing me up, making sure I'm not a crazy person before she introduces herself. I wouldn't blame her. I might have had the same idea if I'd received a message on Facebook from a relative who I didn't know existed. I chew on my thumbnail as I peer over my shoulder, scrutinizing every passerby. What if she doesn't recognize me? I should have sent her a photo.

I'm startled out of my reverie when the chair opposite me scrapes across the floor. A heady waft of perfume — rich, floral, and unmistakably expensive — hits me before the tall, immaculately-dressed woman even speaks. "I take it you're Piper?" she says.

My jaw goes slack at the sight of Callie Madden-Bramston in the flesh. I suddenly feel ridiculous in my chic bohemian outfit. Callie is decked out in white designer workout leggings and a soft, cream-colored velour hoodie. Her face is fully made up and her thick, shiny hair is immaculately curled and falling away from a matching velour headband.

"Er . . . yes," I stammer. "I'm surprised you recognized me."

She rolls her eyes. "Those hideous lips are hard to miss. I fill my top one, but I guess my aesthetician isn't doing that great a job if you detected a resemblance."

"You . . . uh, look amazing," I say, immediately regretting it. It's a lame thing to say, and I cough to cover my awkwardness. "How about some coffee?"

"Sure," Callie replies, pulling out her phone and staring at it. "I'll take a dry grande oat milk cappuccino."

"Okay. Would you like anything to eat with that?"

She glances at me briefly, a bemused look on her face. "From this place? Are you kidding?"

I scramble to my feet, repeating her convoluted coffee order over in my brain. It sounds expensive, and I doubt she has any intention of paying me back, but I'll worry about that later. Marco would say she's taking advantage of me, but, in all fairness, I initiated this meeting, so this one's on me.

I get in line at the counter, glancing back occasionally at Callie, who's sitting with her back to me hunched over her phone. She's acting like this rendezvous is no big deal, while I'm still in a state of complete shock at coming face to face with my biological sister. When I return to the table with drinks in hand, she glances up unsmiling and reaches for hers without a word of thanks. Slipping her phone into her leather crossbody bag, she takes a sip and smacks her highly glossed lips together. "You said you had evidence you're my sister," she says, cocking a manicured brow.

"Yes." I reach into my purse and retrieve the printouts from the website. "It looks like you registered with myancestry.com. That's how they matched us."

Callie takes the pages and pores over them, frowning. After a minute or two, she hands them back without a word.

"I was excited to learn I had a sister," I say, with a sheepish smile.

Callie curls her lip. "I don't know what you're expecting to get out of this, but I'm not in a position to pander to you. My life's complicated enough right now."

Her words cut me to the core. I blink at her, stunned into silence. Is she shutting me out? Rejecting me without even giving me a chance? My fingers shake as I reach for my coffee. "I'm not here to complicate your—"

"Then why are you here?" Callie narrows her eyes at me. "It's odd that you show up right when my stepdaughter goes missing."

15

CHAPTER 5

I choke on my coffee, inadvertently spewing a mouthful all over the table.

Callie screeches back in her chair, staring in horror at her outfit.

"I'm so sorry," I blurt out. "I don't think I got any on you."

"You'd better not have," she snaps, inspecting her sleeves. "This is brand new." She lets out a disgruntled sigh and scoots even further away from the table as if fearing another coffee shower.

"I'm really sorry about your stepdaughter," I say, mopping up the splatter with a napkin. "What's her name?"

"Athena. She's sixteen."

"Do the police have any leads?"

Callie reaches for her cup and twists it around to make sure I haven't polluted it with spittle before taking a sip. She taps a polished fingernail on the plastic lid. "No. They're treating her as a runaway."

"What do you think?"

Callie shrugs. "She wouldn't be the first teenager to run away." She eyes me dubiously. "Have you been talking with her online too?"

"What? No, of course not! I didn't even know you existed until a couple of weeks ago, let alone that you had a step-daughter. Where's her mother?"

"She died of breast cancer."

I grimace as I pick at the cardboard sleeve on my coffee cup. I rack my brain, but I don't recall seeing Athena in any of the photos in Callie's Facebook feed.

"Was Athena unhappy at home?"

The minute the words leave my lips, I wish I could take them back. Callie seems like she would be a difficult person to live with. If Athena was miserable enough to run away, there's a good chance it had something to do with her stepmother.

For the first time, a flicker of fear appears in my sister's eyes. She drops her gaze and sips her oat milk cappuccino. "I've only just met you," she says in a subdued tone. "It doesn't seem appropriate to discuss the situation with you."

I nervously pull at the sleeve of my dress. It sounds like something is seriously amiss in the Bramston household. There are any number of reasons why a sixteen-year-old might be disgruntled, but they don't all run away from home.

"We don't have to talk about it if you don't want to," I say. "But I hope in time we'll grow close enough for you to feel comfortable sharing more of your life with me."

Callie lets out a scoffing laugh. "You may be blood, but you're a stranger. No offense."

Her words sting, but I do my best not to let it show. "I'm not trying to encroach on your life. If you don't want a relationship with me, I'll walk away. I admit I've been stalking you online for days on end. I know you were adopted at birth too, and your parents moved to Florida after they retired. Aren't you in the least bit curious about me?"

Callie smirks. "Sure, why don't you tell me all about your-self, Sis?"

Despite her overtly sarcastic tone, I give her the benefit of the doubt. "I'm thirty-nine years old. Our mother was six-teen when I was born. I was adopted by Glen and Anna Ross.

They were in their late forties when I came into the picture — great parents, but they're both deceased now. I work at a small bakery called—"

"*A bakery?*" Callie blinks at me in a perplexed manner. "Do you own it?"

My cheeks flush. "No. I mostly work behind the counter."

Callie wrinkles her nose in disgust. "Didn't you go to college?"

My palms begin to sweat at the mention of college.

"I did, but . . ." My words trail off and I turn away to compose myself. I don't want to feed my sister a bunch of lies, but this isn't exactly the kind of thing you tell someone the first time you meet them.

"But what?" A gleam of curiosity lights up Callie's eyes. "Did you drop out?"

"No. I graduated from Cal State LA in 2007 with a BA in communications."

"Really? That's where my husband, Lincoln, went to college." Callie inches her chair closer to the table and leans toward me, quirking a questioning brow. "So why are you selling donuts when you have a degree in communications?"

My stomach knots. I didn't anticipate discussing the mistake that derailed my life during our first conversation. I don't know Callie, and I don't know how she'll react. There's a chance she'll reject me for good.

But it's a chance I'll have to take if I want us to become more than a DNA match on a website.

18

CHAPTER 6

My phone beeps and I glance at it, shocked to see that it's already 1:00 p.m. My confessional will have to wait for another day. I'm going to be late getting back to the bakery as it is.

"I'm really sorry," I say, scrambling to my feet. "I need to get back to work." I reach for my cup and scribble my phone number on it. "If you want to continue our chat some other time, give me a call. And if you elect not to, I'm glad we at least got to meet. I hope and pray your stepdaughter shows up safe and well soon."

Callie wiggles her painted fingernails at me by way of goodbye, her face a blank canvas. I can't tell if she's intrigued enough to reach out again, or relieved to see the back of me. Only time will tell.

By the time I get back to the bakery, Jenna is completely frazzled. "Am I ever glad to see you," she wheezes. "It's been insanely busy. We're already sold out of chocolate chip cookies and macaroons."

I dive right into serving the customers patiently waiting in line. The rest of the afternoon flies by and, before I know it, we're wiping down counters and sweeping the floor at the close of the day. As I'm walking out, my phone pings with an incoming message. I'm too hot and sweaty to bother fishing it out of my purse, so I wait until I climb into my car before checking it. My eyes widen in disbelief.

Dinner tonight at 6:30 p.m. We can finish our conversation then. Lincoln is out of town on business. 605 Hawthorne Ave.

I clutch the steering wheel, thinking it over. I'm physically wiped out from work and emotionally spent from the coffee date with my sister earlier. I'm not sure I can handle a second conversation with Callie so soon. But I have a hankering to see inside her house. If it's anything like her wardrobe, it's bound to be worth a visit. Before I can talk myself out of it, I send her a text accepting the invitation.

The minute I get home, I jump in the shower, then go through the arduous process of trying to select another outfit from my dismal clothing collection. I consider putting my bohemian outfit back on but settle for jeans and a long-sleeved cotton shirt — comfort over style.

I have some time to kill before I need to leave, so I call Marco and bring him up to speed.

"Are you sure you want to go to her house?" he asks. "You don't know anything about her. That whole situation with her stepdaughter going missing sounds sketchy, if you ask me. I don't like that she had the gall to ask if you knew anything about it. Be careful. She might be your sister, but she's still a stranger."

"Funny, that's exactly what she said about me. I guess we're going to have to get to know each other before we can trust each other."

There's a long pause before Marco speaks again. "Are you going to tell her?"

"I don't know. I'll see how things go."

Marco grunts. "If you get a bad feeling during dinner, call me. I'll come get you. I don't want you going missing next."

"You worry too much. See you at group."

I end the call and check the time. I need to get going or I'll be late. My stomach roils with nerves. Is it too late to back out now?

As I drive, I replay the conversation with Marco in my mind.

She might be your sister, but she's still a stranger.

I can't ignore a niggling feeling of disquiet. What if Callie really believes I had something to do with her stepdaughter's disappearance?

CHAPTER 7

My eyebrows inch upward as I pull into the tree-lined drive-way of Callie's stately colonial home — the kind of place that screams old money, new renovations, and probably a private chef. I park in the gravel turnaround, and check my appearance in the mirror one last time. A well-dressed couple with a pug exits the equally grand house next door. They give a dismissive nod in my direction as they march off.

Charming. I flash a grin anyway.

I'm already regretting my frumpy outfit choice. If I had a mop and a bucket to accessorize with, I'd look like the help arriving to clean.

At the impressive front door, I ring the bell and admire the intricate black iron scrollwork as I wait for Callie to appear. I can't imagine what a door like this costs — more than my monthly rent. I'm about to press the doorbell a second time, when I hear footsteps approaching from inside. I pull back my shoulders and force my lips into a benign smile as the door swings wide open. Callie's gaze flicks up and down me in one efficient brush stroke conveying disapproval. Her outfit is the exact level of effortlessly expensive I expected: black designer jeans and an off-the-shoulder silk top. Her gleaming curls are artlessly gathered up in a high ponytail — the kind of couture casual look that can only be accomplished with equal shares of time and money.

"I wasn't sure you would show," she says, her tone midway between sardonic and surprised.

I wasn't sure myself until about thirty minutes ago, but I don't intend to acknowledge that.

"Your home is beautiful," I say, stepping into a cavernous travertine foyer.

Callie places one hand on her hip and throws a critical glance down the length of the hallway. "We've just finished an extensive remodel. It was grueling working with the contractor. I would give him explicit instructions, and he would turn around and do the exact opposite. I can't tell you how many times we had to tear something out and start over."

Still jabbering on about her remodeling woes, she leads me to the kitchen. I gape at the gleaming, stainless-steel appliances, truss ceilings and wide plank floor. Light flows effortlessly through the stunning French doors leading out to the back lawn. It's such a breathtaking sight that I don't think I would ever leave if I lived here. I wonder what Lincoln does for a living. From what I've seen so far, I doubt Callie does much of anything, so I'm assuming he's the one who makes the money.

"Something to drink?" Callie asks. "I can open a bottle of Chateau Montesquieu Pinot, or would you prefer a cocktail?"

"Just water for me, please. I don't drink."

Callie spins back around, brows raised. "Are you a health nut, or is there a story there?"

"I'm sure we'll get to it over dinner," I reply. I'm not going to volunteer too much personal information unless she seems willing to reciprocate. By the sound of it, she has plenty of drama of her own — there must be more to the story behind her missing stepdaughter.

While Callie busies herself fixing our drinks, I take another leisurely look around the gleaming kitchen. Disappointingly, I don't detect any enticing smells wafting

23

from the commercial-grade stainless-steel oven. Maybe Callie's idea of dinner is more along the lines of a charcuterie board to go with her expensive-sounding Pinot Noir.

"There you go," she says, placing a glass of water in front of me. She raises her wine glass in a toast. "Here's to sisters."

I clink my glass to hers. "To sisters."

The fleeting smile that appeared on Callie's lips has already disappeared. She's hard to read. I'm not sure she has any real interest in getting to know me, but she invited me here, so she must be hoping to get something out of my visit.

Callie slides onto a bar stool and pats the one next to her. "So, where did we leave off after the introductions? That's right, you were about to explain how you ended up icing cupcakes for a living when you have a communications degree."

I take a sip of water to buy myself a moment. "I'll tell you, but after that it's your turn to share something about your life."

Callie chuckles, expertly swirling the wine in her glass. "Can't say I've missed having a bossy older sister all these years. All right, you go first. Let's get to the interesting stuff."

"I'm a recovering alcoholic."

Callie pulls a face. "Not news. I guessed as much."

I shrug. "Your turn."

She taps a fingernail on the counter, looking pensive. "Hmmm . . . what to choose? Okay, here's something. My husband secretly had a vasectomy and lied to me about having fertility problems."

My jaw drops. The news in itself is shocking, but I'm equally shocked that Callie elected to tell me something so personal and painful right off the bat.

"I'm . . . so sorry," I say, reaching for my water and downing a hasty gulp. "I take it you want a child of your own."

She frowns, looking out through the French doors at the setting sun. "I did, but things are different now."

"How so?"

She turns her head sharply in my direction. "Your turn to answer a question. How'd you become an addict?"

24

I drop my gaze and twist my glass slowly on the counter in front of me. I'll give her something — just not everything. She's still a stranger.

"My best friend, Emma, was assaulted at a college frat party. We were supposed to stick together that night, but I got distracted. I was goofing around with a few of our friends. I had no idea what was happening to Emma upstairs. I fell apart afterward when I found out. Drink helped numb the pain when nothing else could."

Callie scrutinizes me for a long moment as though she senses I'm leaving something important out of the story.

Before she can prod for more details, I pose the question she avoided answering earlier. "Why did Athena run away from home?"

Callie takes a long sip of wine, her eyes never leaving mine. Then she leans over and whispers in my ear.

"You should ask her father that."

CHAPTER 8

I draw in a sharp breath. Is Callie insinuating that Lincoln was abusing his daughter? Or did they just not get along? "What do you mean—"

"Nuh-uh," Callie interrupts. "It's my turn to ask a question."

Before she can get out another word, the doorbell chimes. I startle, knocking over my water glass. "I'm so sorry," I exclaim, jumping up to grab a dishtowel. "That's not your husband, is it?"

Callie rolls her eyes. "Hardly. Lincoln has the entry code."

As she saunters off down the hallway, I grab a towel and clean up the mess.

I've just resumed my seat when she walks back into the kitchen carrying a brown paper bag, the rich, savory scent of something tasty emanating from it.

"I'd be lost without delivery," she laughs, pulling out several cardboard containers. "I don't cook, in case you're wondering. Hope you like Italian."

"Yes! Absolutely." Even though I've eaten enough pasta to last me a lifetime, I'm salivating at the aroma currently tempting my nostrils. Callie dishes us each up a generous serving of the most decadent meal I've laid eyes on in a long time.

"What is this?" I ask, leaning over and inhaling the scent of the sauce.

"Short-rib ravioli — from Trattoria Nonna's. It's one of their specialties. Have you been there?"

"I've never even heard of the place." I dig in and let out a moan of pleasure at the first bite. The meat is succulent, the sauce rich and flavorsome, and the ravioli delicate and fluffy. I'm in heaven.

Callie swallows a mouthful and dabs her napkin carefully around her lips. "Where were we? Oh, that's right, you were about to tell me about your addiction journey." She reaches for the bottle of wine and tops off her glass. "I'm guessing there's more to the story."

She spears a piece of ravioli on her fork and twirls it around, blinking her false lashes at me expectantly.

My heart drums a war beat beneath my ribs. Do I tell her the truth or cement our budding relationship with a lie? I set down my silverware and push my plate to one side. I've suddenly lost my appetite at the thought of talking about it. I let out a long, shuddering sigh.

Callie pops a ravioli into her mouth and chews, giving me her rapt attention. "Go on."

I clear my throat, a cold sweat breaking out along my hairline. All the old familiar feelings of guilt and self-loathing surge through my veins as the memory of that awful day comes flooding back. I would wake up every morning for months afterward praying it was all a bad dream, then spend the days drinking myself into oblivion to try and make the nightmare end — not caring if I killed myself in the process.

Callie gives an annoyed grunt. "You were saying?"

"Emma didn't want to press charges. She'd been drinking and had gone to the party voluntarily. She didn't even know for sure who the guy was who assaulted her. He came from behind and put a hand over her mouth and dragged her into a dark bedroom. She didn't think the police would believe her side of the story. I tried to convince her to report it anyway. I thought I had talked her into it, but then . . ." I trail off, tears prickling my eyes.

"Take a breath," Callie says, casually breaking off a piece of crusty bread from the loaf that came with our meal.

I throw her an irritated look. She's acting like this is some kind of cliffhanger TV series and she's glued to the next episode for entertainment's sake. But this is about a real person, someone I cared about deeply.

I take another sip of water before continuing. "Someone from the party posted a half-naked picture of Emma on the dorm room noticeboard — everyone knew it was her. She . . . she couldn't take it. She killed herself."

Callie freezes, her hand halfway to her mouth. She blinks at me and whispers, "How?"

"She slit her wrists in the bathtub one night after I'd gone to bed. I found her the next morning."

Callie leans back in her chair and lets out a whistle. "That's hardcore. No wonder you're messed up. What a jerk that guy was. And to think he walked away free and clear."

I nod in agreement, even though I still haven't told her what I did afterward. That can wait until another day.

CHAPTER 9

Callie scoots her stool closer to mine. "I'm sorry about your friend. That must have been so hard for you. It's awful being mistreated by a man and being helpless to stop it."

I set down my fork and stare at her in horror. "Callie, is Lincoln abusing you?"

She lets out a thready sigh. "He pushes me around, but he's careful never to leave a mark. Mostly, he manipulates me — psychologically and emotionally. What do you expect when you're married to a trust fund baby? He's always had everything he wanted at his fingertips." She flaps a hand, gesturing at the expansive kitchen. "I mean, look at this place. It reeks of Bramston family money. His father gave him a job — it's not like he earned it. Men like Lincoln, who've never had to work hard a day in their lives, are narcissistic. They think everyone else is there to cater to their wants and needs." She studies her manicured nails. "He's cheated on me twice in the past that I know of, and I think he might be up to his old tricks again."

I give a disgusted shake of my head. "You don't have to put up with it. Leave him."

Callie grimaces. "Believe me, I've thought about it, but I have to be careful. He comes across as very smooth and charming, but he has a dark side. He controls me, and he controls all our money — he made me sign a prenup. If I walk, I leave with nothing but his threats of retribution."

A chill goes through me as Emma's face flashes to mind. I know all about the dark side of men intent on getting what they want at all costs. I won't stand for my sister being abused in that way.

"Are you in danger?" I ask. "Be honest with me, has Lincoln ever physically hurt you?"

"Giving me a black eye is not Lincoln's style. He needs me to look good draped on his arm." She bites her lip, that flicker of fear in her eyes once more. "Can I trust you?"

"One hundred percent," I answer, locking my gaze with hers.

Callie lowers her voice. "I found a stash of photos hidden in a folder at the back of his closet — surveillance-type shots. He's been stalking women."

A trail of short-rib acid rises up my throat. "You have to go to the police. You can't let him get away with it. What if he attacks one of them — or kills them?"

Callie wraps her arms around herself and lets out a soft moan. "What if he already has?"

"What do you mean?"

She shrugs, her eyes downcast.

I grab her and shake her. "What is it? Do you know something? You can't cover for him just because he's your husband."

She raises her head, the hint of tears glistening in her eyes. "What if he's hurt Athena?"

I shrink back in horror. "I can't believe he would harm his own daughter."

Callie blinks back tears. "What if she'd discovered what he was doing and threatened to go to the authorities? He might have lashed out in anger. A man like Lincoln would do anything to avoid prison. He's a narcissist. You have no idea what he's capable of." She eyes me hesitantly. "There's something else I need to tell you."

30

I squirm on my stool. I'm not sure I'm up for any more dark revelations about Callie's life. It seems all the money in the world hasn't afforded her any happier an existence than I have. I may not have Bramston-level wealth or success, but I have the best boss in the world, and a friend who would go to the ends of the earth for me.

Callie picks at the sleeve of her sweater. "Remember I told you Lincoln went to Cal State LA too?"

I nod, wondering where she's going with this.

"He graduated the same year as you — 2007."

My pulse begins to pound in my temples. I try not to connect the dots but they're jumping out at me regardless.

"I found a photograph of a partially clothed woman in that folder of Lincoln's. She was wearing Cal State LA sweatpants." Callie wets her lips. "There's a name on the back of the photo."

CHAPTER 10

"What's the name?" I whisper, my stomach curdling with fear.

"Emma," Callie chokes out.

For a long moment, I sit frozen in my seat, digesting the shock. I want to ask her to let me see the photo, but the words stick in my throat. It must be a coincidence. Surely Lincoln can't be the monster who attacked Emma and drove her into an early grave. I haven't even met my sister's husband yet, but hatred for him is already fermenting in my veins. I'm not sure I'll be able to keep myself from scratching his eyes out when we finally meet.

I take a deep, calming breath and try to think rationally, like Marco would tell me to do. There's a strong possibility this is just a freaky coincidence. As much as I dread doing it, I need to examine the evidence before I rush to judgment. "Let me see the photo," I say.

Callie opens her mouth to respond but freezes at the sound of the front door opening.

My eyes jerk in the direction of the door. "Who's that?"

She presses a trembling fist to her mouth. "Lincoln must have come home early."

Seconds later, a tall, good-looking man in his forties strides into the kitchen. He comes to a sudden halt at the sight of me. His steel-gray eyes swerve from Callie to me, then back. "Who's this?"

"Lincoln, darling, meet my sister, Piper," Callie replies in an overly cheerful tone.

Lincoln scowls. "You don't have a sister." His eyes travel up and down the length of me as though examining something repulsive. He turns away and addresses Callie. "I need to speak to you in private, now."

She throws me an apologetic look, then corrects her face to neutral as she slides down from her stool and follows her husband out of the kitchen. I flinch when I hear a door slam. I need to make sure my sister's safe. I get to my feet and pad across the kitchen floor and out into the hall. The door opposite the kitchen is closed, so I tiptoe across and press my ear to it.

"What's she doing here?" Lincoln growls.

"I told you, she's my sister," Callie responds. "She found me on myancestry.com."

"So she says. You have no idea who she is. Judging by the way she's dressed, she doesn't have two nickels to rub together. She's probably some scam artist who found you online and is targeting you for money."

"She showed me the paperwork from the website. She's definitely my biological sister."

Lincoln lets out a grunt of disgust. "It doesn't change the fact that she's after money. You would know all about that."

"Seriously? Is that all you ever think about?" Callie's voice rises an octave. "What about the woman you're sleeping with? Is she only after your money too?"

"What are you talking about?" Lincoln snaps.

"I know you're having an affair. Is it our neighbor this time? I've seen you whispering with Vanessa when you don't think I'm around."

"Don't be ridiculous. You're being paranoid."

I quietly shift my weight and retreat a step from the door. I wonder if Vanessa is the well-dressed woman I saw leaving the house next door with her husband and dog. They looked like a happily married couple to me, but appearances can be deceptive.

I can't risk eavesdropping any longer. The conversation between Callie and Lincoln is growing more heated by the second. One or the other of them might burst through the door at any minute.

I barely make it back to the relative safety of my bar stool before the door flies open and I hear Lincoln yell, "Get her out of here, now!"

Callie trudges back into the kitchen. She shakes her head at me. "He's impossible. He's insisting you leave. I'm sorry."

I reach for my purse without a word. I have no desire to be in the house with a violent man, let alone one who stalks and attacks women, and might have assaulted Emma. I only wish I could persuade Callie to come with me. She'd be better off walking away from the money and starting over. Maybe I'm naive, but with Lincoln out of the picture, I can't help thinking our relationship would have a real chance.

Only problem is, getting away from a powerful man is easier said than done.

CHAPTER 11

I pull into the parking lot at Brentdale Presbyterian Church, where the weekly AA meeting I attend takes place. It's been two days since Lincoln kicked me out and I haven't heard a breath from Callie. I've been mulling everything over and have come to the conclusion that she might be right to suspect Lincoln of harming his daughter. He does seem prone to anger. I did a little research online and found a couple of articles about Athena Bramston's disappearance. There weren't too many details. She went to bed one night and was gone by the following morning. Callie was out of town for a few days and Athena was alone in the house with her father.

The police are classifying her as a runaway, but I can't shake Callie's suspicions from my mind. I've been so discombobulated, I actually thought about skipping group tonight. But Marco and I made a pact a long time ago never to stand each other up. After a decade of friendship, we haven't broken that promise yet.

I lock my car and head down to the church basement where we usually gather. There's something safe and comfortable about this place — a hidden refuge of sorts. It's like coming home. It was scary attending that first night. I'd made a lot of assumptions

— none of them good. I sat in my car in the parking lot for a good twenty minutes fighting the urge to drive away and down a bottle of vodka. In the end, I convinced myself to go inside. My legs were like noodles. I wasn't ready to get up in front of everyone and announce my name and confess my sins. But it turned out to be a safe space, and I slowly began to relax. The topic that first night was "accepting what can't be changed." It hit me hard because I had never really accepted what happened to Emma, which was the catalyst to my drunken downfall.

I remember being intimidated by some of the attendees — in particular, an enormous bald guy with a plethora of tattoos. At one point, he shared his story about losing custody of his two young daughters because of his drinking — he sobbed like a baby the whole time. It was a good reminder not to make assumptions about people before getting to know them — like Callie. She's a bird with broken wings beneath the designer clothing.

"Hey, Piper!" Marco calls out to me when I walk into the meeting room.

I give him a hug and plop down in the plastic chair next to him.

"How did it go at Callie's?" he asks.

I twist my lips. "Not as well as I'd hoped."

The crease between his brows deepens. "Personality clash?"

I glance around at the other participants taking their seats as John, our chairperson, gets ready to begin the AA preamble.

"It's complicated," I whisper. "Let's grab some food afterward, and I'll tell you all about it."

* * *

A couple of hours later, Marco and I are seated at his kitchen table digging into cartons of kung po beef and prawn chop suey and loading up our plates.

"So," he says, waving his chopsticks at me. "What's the scoop on your sister?"

36

"She's rich, for starters. Seriously rich." I swallow a mouthful of rice and chicken. "I mean, everyone's richer than you when you're earning minimum wage, but believe me, she's loaded. At least, her husband, Lincoln, is. He's a trust fund baby."

"So, what's the problem?" Marco asks.

I scrunch my napkin in my fist. "Her husband is the problem."

Marco chuckles. "A bit tight-fisted, is he?"

I stare at him until the smile fades from his face.

"What?" he asks, setting down a carton of rice and giving me his full attention.

"Callie thinks Lincoln had something to do with his daughter's disappearance."

CHAPTER 12

Marco rubs a hand over his jaw. "Tell me you're joking."

"I wish I were. Lincoln's daughter, Athena, has been missing for almost a week now."

Marco shoves his paper plate aside, shaking his head in disbelief. "You've only just met your sister and the first thing she tells you is that she suspects her husband of harming his daughter — what evidence does she have? How do you know his daughter's even missing?"

"I checked the story out online. She vanished during the night from her house. By all appearances, she left voluntarily. The police think she's a runaway. But Callie's not so sure. She says Lincoln has a dark side."

"What's that supposed to mean?"

"She says he's abusive and manipulative, and she thinks he's having an affair with a neighbor. He's cheated on her before."

Marco's expression morphs into one of distaste. "So he's a jerk. Doesn't mean he'd harm his own daughter."

"Callie thinks he's capable of it. She found a folder at the back of his closet with a bunch of surveillance-type photos. It looks like he's been stalking women. She's afraid Athena might have discovered what he was up to and threatened to expose him."

Marco's brows shoot upward. "Your sister needs to turn those photos over to the police."

"She wants to, but she's scared Lincoln will retaliate." I peer into the carton of food in front of me and stab half-heartedly at a prawn. "That's not the worst of it. She also found a photo of a half-naked woman wearing Cal State LA sweatpants. There was a name on the back of it — *Emma*." I lock eyes with Marco. "Lincoln was attending Cal State the same year Emma was assaulted."

Marco lets out a low whistle and rubs a hand over his head. "I don't like where this is going. Did she show you the photo?"

"She was about to, but Lincoln came back early from a business trip and kicked me out of the house."

"He sounds charming." Marco folds his arms in front of his chest. "You need to have Callie show you those photos. And if what she's saying is true, go to the police. You don't want what happened to Emma happening to other women."

"I'm still hoping it's not her. It's too horrific to think that Lincoln — my own brother-in-law — might be the man who assaulted her."

"No sense speculating until you confirm it. If it is her, then finding your sister was meant to be. You can't get justice for Emma, but you can turn Lincoln in for stalking those other women and rescue your sister from his clutches in the process. And if he did do away with his daughter — which I highly doubt — it's bound to come out in the investigation."

I nod, thinking it through. "I need to move quickly. I'm afraid something might happen to Callie too. If Lincoln finds out she's discovered his photo stash, there's no telling what he'll do."

"You have to be smart about this, Piper. The Bramston family will have expensive lawyers on retainers. You can't make accusations without evidence."

"I won't involve the police until I have the photos."

Marco shoots me a look of alarm. "You can't take them. If you alert Lincoln to what you're doing, it might put your sister in harm's way. Take some pictures of them with your phone. That should be enough for the police to get a search warrant."

A shiver runs across my shoulders. "I'm afraid of what else they might find in the house."

Marco rubs a hand awkwardly over my back. "I doubt he has his daughter stashed in a freezer in the basement, if that's what you're worried about."

I give a wan smile, halfway heartened by Marco's logic.

But a nagging feeling in the pit of my stomach tells me Lincoln could go to any lengths to hide his dark obsession.

CHAPTER 13

I message Callie the following morning asking her to call me, but it's several days later before her number pops up on my phone. I dust the flour from my hands on my apron and dash into the bathroom at work to take the call.

"Are you okay?" I blurt out. "I was worried something might have happened to you."

"I'm fine. Just keeping a low profile. Lincoln doesn't want me to have anything more to do with you. He thinks you're trying to worm your way into our lives for money."

A twinge of guilt goes through me. I wouldn't turn down a generous gift from my wealthy sister — enough to cover a month's rent would be nice — but I can hardly admit to it. "I need to take a look at those photos you found," I say. "I want to see if I recognize the girl from Cal State LA."

There's an extended silence before Callie responds. "Okay, meet me at Highland Park at noon. I don't want to go back to the mall in case someone spots me there with you and mentions it to Lincoln."

I grimace as I check the time — eleven forty. Even if I leave right away, there's no way I can make it to the park by noon. Besides, I don't have time to take lunch today. We're swamped and I can't leave Jenna to deal with the crowd alone. "I don't get off until five. I can be there by five thirty."

Callie sighs dramatically. "Fine. I'll be at the playground. Don't be late. Lincoln will be home by six thirty. We have a function to attend tonight."

I have a hard time focusing on work for the remainder of my shift and, after messing up two customers' orders, Jenna pulls me aside. "Is everything okay, Piper?"

"Yes, I'm fine, thanks. Just tired. I didn't sleep too well again."

"Are you worried about your landlord increasing the rent?" Jenna squints at me. "Do you need an advance? Be honest. You know I'm happy to help."

My cheeks flush. I've had to humble myself and ask for an advance more times than I care to admit. It's embarrassing, not to mention nerve-racking, perpetually living on the edge of financial ruin. "Thank you, but no. I'm good."

"Then go on home and get some rest," Jenna says. "The rush is over now. I've got it from here."

I undo my apron, trying to quell the waves of guilt I'm wrestling with. I hate lying to my boss, but I can't jeopardize my sister's safety by involving anyone else in this situation until Lincoln is safely behind bars. Until then, the less Jenna knows, the better.

I end up clocking out twenty minutes early. It doesn't leave me enough time to go home and change before I meet Callie, so I drive straight to the park and wait in my car until a white Tesla pulls up beside me. My sister climbs out, and I scramble out of my Camry after her. She narrows her eyes at me, then turns and marches over to a bench behind the climbing frame. I sit down next to her, hands stuffed deep into my pockets.

I throw a fleeting glance around. "Did you bring them?" I ask in a choked whisper. This feels like a scene from a movie where I'm buying government secrets from a spy.

Wordlessly, Callie digs in her white Kate Spade tote bag and passes me an envelope.

My fingers shake as I slide the photos out. Trancelike, I shuffle through them, stunned by the invasion of privacy. There's no doubt Lincoln was stalking these women. They obviously had no idea they were being photographed as they walked along the street or climbed into a car. Some of the photos are blurry, but in others I can make out a partial side profile — not enough to identify them. When I reach the bottom of the stack, I peek inside the envelope to make sure I haven't missed any. "Where's the one of Emma?" I ask.

Callie bites her lip. "Gone. He must have taken it."

"What?" I eye her suspiciously. "Why would he do that?"

She nibbles nervously on her thumbnail, darting a glance around as though fearful Lincoln might be eavesdropping. "You're in danger, Piper."

I breathe slowly in and out. "What do you mean?"

She leans over and mutters, "He recognized you. He knows you were Emma's friend."

CHAPTER 14

I stare at Callie agape. "Are you sure?"

She gives a stiff nod. "He was acting very oddly after you left — asked me a bunch of questions about you. When I pulled the folder of pictures out of his closet this morning, the photo of the girl from Cal State LA was gone. He's either hidden it somewhere else or destroyed it."

I squeeze my hands together in my lap. It must have been Emma. Why else would Lincoln have gotten rid of the evidence? And it explains his animosity toward me. I don't remember his face from the frat party that night, but there is something disturbing about him.

"I need to take a few pictures of these," I say, pulling out my phone and snapping away as I shuffle through the photos.

Callie flashes me a startled look. "What are you going to do with them?"

"The responsible thing," I reply in a testy tone. "I'm going to turn them over to the police — like you should have done. It's clear Lincoln's been stalking these women — they have no idea they're in danger."

"You don't understand who you're going up against," Callie says, fidgeting with the zipper on her purse. "Lincoln's parents have deep pockets and a far reach."

"So? They're hardly going to hire a hitman to do away with me, are they?"

Callie arches an expertly shaped brow. "They'll do whatever is necessary to make this go away. You're a nobody in the Bramston world — I'm a nobody too, for that matter."

I furrow my brow. "What about Athena? She's not a nobody. If she found out what Lincoln was up to, it gives him a motive to get rid of her. Surely Athena's grandparents care enough about her not to get in the way of an investigation to find out what happened to her?"

Callie shrugs. "Eleanor and Theo believe what the police believe — she ran away. At least, that's what they're telling me. You'll never convince them that Lincoln had anything to do with it. In their eyes, he can do no wrong."

"Have you considered the possibility Athena might have run away? Maybe Lincoln had nothing to do with it after all."

"It's possible," Callie says, sounding dubious. "But he doesn't seem too bothered about finding her."

"Maybe there's something we can do."

"What?"

"I don't know," I admit. "Hand out flyers, put up posters — that kind of thing."

I glance at my watch. "You need to get going. I'll call the police when I get home and make arrangements to show them these photos. I'll let you know how it goes."

As I get to my feet, Callie grabs me by the arm, latching on tightly. "Be careful, Piper. I don't want anything to happen to you now that I've found you."

I lean over and hug her, tears pricking my eyes. It feels as though we're beginning to bond as I'd hoped. "I'll be in touch," I say, releasing her. I wave briefly before striding away from the park bench and back to my car.

On the drive home, my thoughts drift to my missing niece. I need to do something to help find her — especially since those responsible for her disappearance may very well be the ones covering it up.

* * *

Just as I put the key in my apartment door, a voice whispers in my ear, "Don't scream. Walk calmly inside."

I do as I'm told on trembling legs. The front door slams behind me and I swivel to see Lincoln Bramston standing in the dingy space. Everything Callie said about him flashes to mind. He's a sick, violent man. I need to stay calm and try to talk my way out of this. "What do you want?" I ask trying to keep my tone level. "Is Callie okay?"

He snorts. "You tell me. You just had a conversation with her."

I shift nervously from one foot to the other. "How do you know?"

Lincoln gives a sardonic laugh. "My wife can't make a move without me knowing about it. What were you two talking about?"

"It's none of your business."

He takes a menacing step toward me, his face twisting in an ugly scowl. "We'll see about that."

Instinctively, I slam my hands on his chest and shove him backward. "I know what you did to Emma!" I scream. "It was you, wasn't it? You're the one who assaulted her and posted that picture in the dorm room. She killed herself because of you!"

"I have no idea what you're talking about!"

"Then why did you follow me here? You're guilty and you know it. You recognized me!"

"I came here to warn you to stay out of my wife's life." He throws a scathing glance around my meager abode. "By the look of things, you need money in a bad way. I know

46

your type. You'll try and wheedle as much as possible out of Callie, and when that doesn't satisfy you, you'll concoct some bogus lawsuit."

"You've got me all wrong," I say. "I have no interest in suing you, as satisfying as it might be. But I care about what you did to Emma. And I know about the stalking. I have copies of the photos you took. I'm going to make sure the whole world knows just how sick and twisted you are."

His dark eyes fill with rage. "So, this is about blackmail. I knew you'd be trouble. Did you take my daughter?" He grabs my neck and begins to squeeze. My eyes bulge as I stare up at the bare lightbulb in the ceiling, my thoughts jumbling together like a load of laundry. How can the bulb be burned out already when I only replaced it last week?

Before I can rationalize it, darkness takes over.

CHAPTER 15

When I come to, it takes me a moment to remember where I am. I blink up at the bare bulb in the ceiling and slowly ease myself into a sitting position. Pain radiates down my neck, and I instinctively move my hands to massage it. Lincoln must have squeezed until I passed out. Did he think he'd killed me? Was that his intention? Or was he just trying to scare me?

My mind jumps to Callie. She's not safe either. I need to call her and warn her. A surge of adrenaline spurs me to my feet. I dig around in my purse for my phone. It rings and rings, then goes to voicemail. My thoughts plummet to the worst possible scenario. *Lincoln went on a rampage. I'm too late to save her.* Panicked, I try her number again. To my relief, she answers this time.

"Callie! Are you okay?" I wheeze.

"I'm fine," she replies sounding confused. "What's wrong with your voice?"

"Lincoln attacked me."

"What?" Callie gasps. "Are you okay?"

"I think so. He was waiting for me outside my apartment. I told him I knew what he'd done and that I was going to the police. He choked me until I passed out. When I came to, he was gone. How did he know where I lived?"

"I have no idea. I don't even know where you live. But Lincoln's an expert at stalking women."

"Is he there right now?"

"No. Did you call the cops?"

"Not yet. He's probably on his way home. Go next door to your neighbors. Text me when Lincoln gets there. I want to make sure he's there when the cops show up."

"Are you sure you're okay? Do you need me to drive you to the hospital?"

I try swallowing to make sure I still can. If circumstances were different, I might take her up on her offer. But I don't have medical insurance and I can't afford the luxury of a precautionary checkup. "No, I'm fine. My throat's just a bit raw."

"I'm so sorry," Callie says in a subdued tone. "I knew you were in danger the minute I realized that photo of Emma was gone."

"It's not me you need to worry about anymore. I'm locked inside my apartment. You need to get out of your house."

I end the call and get up to examine my neck more closely in the bathroom mirror. Surprisingly, it's only a little red — no fingermarks. Callie was right — Lincoln's clever about hiding what he does. What if I go to the police and he denies everything? His expensive lawyers might threaten to sue me for making a false report. I check my phone repeatedly, anxiously waiting on Callie's text. I assume Lincoln's headed home. Callie mentioned something about a function tonight.

Still shaken up, I head into the kitchen and pour myself a glass of water. I'm thankful I don't have alcohol in the apartment anymore. I'm pretty sure I would break down and drink myself into oblivion to calm my nerves. I can't even call Marco for support because he'll try to play the hero and charge right over to Lincoln's house to confront him. I grab the remote and turn the television on, then flick aimlessly through the channels for a few minutes before settling on a wildlife documentary. In a matter of minutes, my eyelids are drooping.

I almost jump out of my skin when my phone rings. Jenna's number appears on the screen. I rub a hand across my brow, disoriented at first until I realize how late it is. Shock blazes through me. I've been asleep for hours, with no word from Callie. I can't take Jenna's call right now. She's probably going to ask me to go in early tomorrow — it's the only reason she ever calls this late. What am I supposed to tell her? *My brother-in-law's a predator*. I suppose I could tell her I'm sick. My finger hovers over the 'accept call' button but, before I press it, another call comes in from Callie. Heart pumping, I send Jenna's call to voicemail and accept Callie's.

"Is he back?" I ask.

"He's dead!" my sister sobs into the phone. "Lincoln's dead."

CHAPTER 16

My brain can't compute what Callie's saying. It's incomprehensible that the man who tried to strangle me only a few hours earlier is dead. Did he have a heart attack, or was it some kind of accident?

"Calm down, Callie, and tell me what happened," I say in as soothing a voice as I can muster.

"I don't know. I . . . I found him at the bottom of the stairs. I heard arguing and then this loud thump."

My brain feels sluggish. None of this is making sense. "Did someone break in?"

"I don't know."

"Did you see anyone leaving the house?"

"No," she wails. "I don't know what to do."

I snatch up my purse and keys, trying to gather my thoughts into some semblance of order. All I know for sure is that my sister needs me. "I'm on my way. Don't touch anything."

I almost pull over several times on the drive to Callie's house. I feel sick to my stomach at the thought of Lincoln's lifeless body lying at the bottom of their staircase. It's not as though I don't think he deserved it after everything he's done — I've wished every kind of death on Emma's attacker a thousand times over. But Callie's story of what happened makes me uneasy. The person Lincoln was likely arguing with in his house this evening is his wife. Is it possible Callie confronted him about assaulting me and they got into a fight about it?

She could have accidentally pushed him down the stairs and made up the story about an intruder. Or perhaps someone really did come into the house and attack Lincoln. Men like Lincoln always have enemies. Did the next-door neighbor find out Lincoln was having an affair with his wife and confront him? Myriad possibilities run through my head — all speculation.

My thoughts turn to Athena. An icy shiver goes through me. If Lincoln did have something to do with his daughter's disappearance, we might never find out what happened to her now that he's dead. I can't believe he's really dead. I can still see the rage blazing in his eyes. I barely knew the man, but I won't miss him. Still, I hope for Callie's sake she had nothing to do with his demise. Vigilante justice will come back to bite her — something I know all too well.

It's almost midnight by the time I pull into her driveway. I don't want to ring the doorbell and listen to it chime all the way through the house like a death knell. Instead, I shoot her a text to let her know I'm here, then hurry up the stone steps to the front door. She pulls it open and peers hesitantly out at me. I can barely contain my shock at her bedraggled appearance. Her hair is a tangled nest, and her alabaster cheeks are streaked with mascara. She shoots a nervous glance over my shoulder. "You didn't call the police, did you?"

I shake my head as I step inside the foyer. "You didn't touch anything, did you?"

"No." She wraps her arms around herself and drops her head. "I can't bring myself to go near him."

I glance across the cavernous foyer at the dark shape lying at the bottom of the staircase. "How do you know he's dead?"

She purses her lips. "Go look for yourself."

I pull back my shoulders and tiptoe across the foyer as though I might wake him. But the minute I'm standing over him, I realize that's never going to happen. I'm no medical expert, but it looks like he's broken his neck in the fall. His eyes are wide open, his lifeless gaze positioned on the custom polished-walnut handrail that failed to save him. I tent my hands over my nose and mouth and take a few deep breaths, before walking back over to Callie. "We should cover him. Do you have a blanket or a throw or something?"

She gestures with her chin to the family room off to the left. "In there."

"Don't just stand there. Go get it," I bark, not bothering to curb my irritation at her practiced helplessness.

She narrows her eyes at me but trots off and fetches an oversized throw. "I can't do it," she says, thrusting it at me before folding her arms in front of her chest again and turning her back on her dead husband. I quickly take care of the undesirable task, then make sure the front door is locked, before accompanying Callie to the kitchen.

"Put some coffee on," I say, gesturing to the stainless-steel espresso machine dominating the counter. "We need to talk about what we're going to do with the body."

CHAPTER 17

Callie wrinkles her brow. "Won't the EMT's take care of Lincoln's body?"

"Not if he was murdered by his wife."

She stares at me open-mouthed. "What are you saying? I didn't kill Lincoln. I told you I was in bed when it happened. I gave up on him coming home tonight — I figured he was with another woman. When I woke up, I heard him arguing with someone, and then there was a loud crash. I'm guessing that's when the intruder shoved him down the stairs."

I eye her skeptically. "You're not fooling me, Callie. There was no intruder. No one broke into your house. Where's the evidence? No broken glass, no kicked-in door, no blaring alarm."

She blinks rapidly at me. "It mightn't have been a stranger. It could have been our neighbor, Doug. Lincoln would have opened the door for him if he'd come over. Doug might have found out that Lincoln and Vanessa were carrying on behind his back."

I tap my fingers on the table, my brain screaming at me to make sense of it. "You said you heard arguing. Wouldn't you have recognized Doug's voice?"

Callie shakes her head. "It was muffled. I had my earplugs in. I was trying to sleep. And my bedroom door was closed. But I could tell it was a man arguing with Lincoln. Doug had an axe to grind with him so he's the most likely suspect."

I furrow my brow. "It doesn't make sense. Why would Lincoln invite him upstairs?"

"I don't know," Callie says, throwing up her hands. "Maybe Doug chased him up there."

I pin a scathing gaze on her, trying to curb my frustration. The story is becoming less believable by the minute. "Callie, I can't help you if you don't come clean and tell me the truth about what happened. The only two people who were here tonight were you and Lincoln, and he isn't talking."

Her bottom lip begins to wobble. She fiddles with the coffee maker for a minute or two before her eyes pool with tears. "It . . . was an accident."

Goosebumps prick my arms. "Go on," I say in a measured tone.

"I told Lincoln I'd found the photos and that I knew he'd assaulted you. He was furious — threw me up against the wall and punched me in the stomach. He'd been drinking, he was out of control. I told him he wasn't going to get away with abusing me anymore. I was going to leave him and report it." She pulls out a tissue and dabs at her nose. "He laughed at me — said he would destroy me, just like he'd destroyed every other woman who'd crossed him. I don't know what came over me. I ran at him, screaming. It took him by surprise. He was standing at the top of the staircase, and he went flying backward. I remember hearing 'thunk' after 'thunk' as he hit the stairs on the way down." She buries her face in her hands, her shoulders heaving up and down. "He didn't move again after that."

I scrunch my eyes shut, trying to blot out the horrific image in my mind of Lincoln tumbling down the staircase to his death. I can relate to Callie's rage, but I can't get caught up in the emotion of it all. I need to be rational and think things through. If it really was an accident. Callie doesn't deserve to go to prison. The problem is, not everyone will feel that way. If Lincoln's parents are half as influential as Callie says they are, she won't stand a chance against their legal prowess.

I get to my feet and wrap my sister in a hug. Her tiny yoga-toned frame trembles in my arms. "We'll figure this out," I assure her. "First things first, we're going to need that caffeine."

While she brews the coffee, I make a trip to the bathroom and give myself a pep talk in the mirror. One of us has to stay strong, and Callie isn't currently up to the challenge. The confident, sophisticated persona she projected when we first met has crumbled in the face of adversity. The recovered alcoholic will have to stand in the gap.

When I return to the kitchen, she's seated at the table with two steaming mugs of coffee in front of her. "I don't want to go to prison," she says in a little-girl-lost voice as I pull out the chair next to her.

I reach for my mug and take a sip. She wouldn't last a night. That's why I need to come up with a plan to make this go away.

CHAPTER 18

Callie lifts her mug to her lips, but her hand is trembling so much she sloshes coffee over the side and onto the table. I jump up and grab a paper towel.

"I should have called 911 right away," she says, shaking her head. "I don't know why I called you first. I guess I'm afraid of Lincoln's parents — they'll never accept that this was an accident." She takes a ragged breath. "But I feel stronger now you're here. I know I need to call the cops. The longer I wait, the more guilty I look."

She reaches for her phone on the table, but I snatch it up before she gets ahold of it. "Wait! We need to talk about this first."

Callie rumples her forehead. "Why? What is there to talk about?"

"It's complicated," I say, scrunching up the sodden paper towel in my fist. "There are things about me you don't know — things that could jeopardize you in this situation."

"Like what?"

I let out a resigned sigh. "It goes back to when I was in college. I didn't tell you the whole story about what happened after Emma was assaulted."

Callie remains motionless, a laser-like gaze trained on me.

I suck in a silent breath, hoping I can get through my story without breaking down. "A couple of months after Emma died, Brad Halstead, one of the guys who was at the frat party that night, started harassing me. He knew I was Emma's friend, and he enjoyed taunting me. He caught up with me late one evening on campus and said he had something to show me. Before I realized what was happening, he had pulled up his sweatshirt. He was wearing a T-shirt underneath with the half-naked photo of Emma printed on it." I pause for a heartbeat, my mind flashing back to that awful moment. "I couldn't take it anymore. Something exploded inside me. I did the same thing you did tonight. I went ballistic and shoved him. He fell backwards down the stone steps we were standing on." I bite my lip, determined not to cry. "He was so still, at first, I thought I'd killed him. But it was worse — much worse. Turned out he was paralyzed from the neck down. I left him a vegetable." I pause, the threat of tears scalding my eyes. "I went to prison for eighteen months and Brad got life in a full-time care facility."

Callie's voice quiets to a whisper. "But . . . it was an accident."

"Yes, but Brad's dad was a judge. Sometimes it's not so much the facts that matter, it's the power and influence of the people involved. And by the sound of it, Lincoln's parents have plenty of both." I fix an earnest gaze on Callie. "That's why you can't involve the police in this. They'll think you got the idea to kill your husband from me."

CHAPTER 19

"Don't you think the police will believe me if we tell them Lincoln assaulted you?" Callie asks, her voice plaintive and scared. "I can show them the photos I found in his closet. Surely they'll understand why I lashed out."

"It's still going to strike them as odd that only a few days after we connect, you 'accidentally' shove your husband down a flight of stairs. They're going to suspect you did exactly what I did to punish a man who was abusing you." I take a swig of my coffee, trying to gauge her reaction. She stares morosely at a spot on the floor in front of her. I'm not sure if I'm getting through to her. There is no way this ends well for either of us if she calls the police.

"Even if they do believe your side of the story," I go on, "like you said yourself, Lincoln's parents won't buy it. They'll do everything in their power to make sure this goes to trial. Are you willing to risk going to prison? I can tell you right now you'll never make it on the inside."

Callie chews on her thumbnail, a stricken look in her eyes. "So, what are we going to do?"

It doesn't escape my notice that she now considers me an equal partner in her dilemma. And she might be right. There's a good chance the police will think I was in cahoots with her, or they might even suspect me of taking care of business on her behalf. It doesn't look good for either of us. However we get out of this mess, I'm going to have to be the one to come up with a solution.

"We have to make it look like a suicide," I say with the conviction of someone who knows what they're talking about. But I don't. I'm making it up as I go along. Marco might have a better idea, but I can't drag him into this.

Callie twirls a strand of hair around her finger. "I don't know. I've never heard of anyone committing suicide by throwing themselves down a staircase."

"That's not what I meant. The suicide can't take place in the house. We can't have you anywhere near the scene."

Callie's mascara-ringed eyes widen in horror. "Are you saying we have to move him?"

I give a grim nod. "There's no way around it. The most convincing scenario will be to make it look like he drove off the side of the road."

Callie frowns. "But why would the police think it was a suicide and not an accident?"

"Because we're going to write a suicide note. Think about it. You found out his dirty little secret and confronted him about the photos, the stalking, the assaults, the affair, possibly even getting rid of his daughter. He couldn't bear the thought of everyone knowing what he'd done, especially not his parents. It's not unreasonable to think he would take the coward's way out rather than face a trial and prison."

Callie fidgets in her chair, her eyes not meeting mine. She seems scared of Lincoln's reach, even in death. I need her to commit to the plan. Every minute we waste is more time for rigor mortis to set in, which will only make our job more difficult. "Callie, are you with me?"

She gives a barely perceptible nod. "Okay."

"Good." I get to my feet. "We'll start by writing a suicide note on Lincoln's computer. Do you have any gloves?"

She fetches a box of latex gloves from a supply cupboard and we each don a pair before entering Lincoln's office. Callie types in the password and, a moment later, the screen lights up.

"What are you thinking?" she asks. "Should the note be left for me?"

"Yes, but we can't alert anyone to the fact that he's dead just yet. Leave it as a draft message in his email. When he doesn't return home tonight, you can call the police — let their digital forensic experts find it."

She wets her lips nervously. "Do I have to write it?"

"You know him best. You can do this, Callie. You're not going to let me down, are you? I'm risking everything to help you."

"I know you are, and I appreciate it. I really do." A lone tear trickles down her cheeks. "It's just that I don't know what—"

"It's okay. We'll come back to it later," I interrupt, in a bid to circumvent a breakdown. "Let's focus on getting the body out of here first. I need you to turn off the exterior security cameras and delete the footage. We'll roll Lincoln onto a blanket and drag him out to the garage."

Standing over his body a short time later, I take a deep breath. There's no coming back from what we're about to do. But what's the alternative? I can't let my sister go to prison, and I can't stomach the thought of going back.

CHAPTER 20

With significant effort, mostly on my part, we manage to roll Lincoln's dead weight up in a blanket. Dragging him all the way to the garage proves more difficult than I anticipated. The blanket keeps coming undone and we resort to tying a rope around it to keep him inside. There's a sickening thump as we haul him down the steps from the kitchen into the garage. It sounded like his skull cracking on concrete, not that it makes a difference at this point. The worst has already been done.

Callie sobs quietly the entire time, lending me only sporadic help with the physical side of things. By the time I manage to drag Lincoln over to his silver Mercedes S class on the far side of the garage, I'm sweating profusely, even though it's dark and frigid as a tomb out here. Callie stands frozen in place, waiting for me to do the heavy lifting and somehow maneuver her dead husband into the car. Her pale, mascara-streaked cheeks highlighted by the dim light of my iPhone lend her the freakish appearance of a doll from a horror movie. She's giving me the creeps, but I don't want to risk turning on any more lights than necessary. The more inconspicuous we are, the better.

"Don't just stand there. You're going to have to help me," I say, waving Callie over. "He's too much dead weight for me to lift by myself. We'll put him in the back seat for now until you reach the area where you'll dump the car."

Callie comes to an abrupt standstill. "I'm not driving a dead body around. You can't ask me to do that. It's unnatural."

I blow a strand of hair out of my face as I yank open the back door of the Mercedes. I was planning on following her in my car, but I guess it won't do any harm to leave my Camry here. "Fine, take your car. I'll drive the Mercedes. Now get over here and help me push him inside."

I'm trying not to be the one who falls apart, but my insides feel like an earthquake rumbling beneath the surface. Marco's face flashes to mind again, and a pang of guilt hits. He would be devastated if he knew the decisions I'm making tonight, but I'm in too far now to reverse course. I'm putting everything I've worked so hard for in jeopardy. But not for selfish reasons. I'm trying to spare my sister the horrors of life behind bars. I've only just found her. I don't want to spend the next few decades visiting her in prison — nor sharing a cell with her.

Callie blinks dubiously at Lincoln's rolled up body. "What should we do about the blanket?"

"Leave it for now," I say. "Grab ahold of a corner and help me get him into the car."

It takes a few tries, but we finally manage to heave Lincoln's upper body onto the back seat of the Mercedes. I go around to the other side and pull him all the way in. It's dark enough that, at first glance, no one would ever suspect I'm transporting a body. But there'll be no denying it if we're stopped for any reason. I shine my iPhone flashlight around the garage and spot a pile of folded drop cloths in one corner. I could throw them over the body, but it might look more suspicious than the blanket. I'm pretty sure there aren't too many painters driving around in a Mercedes S class with stained drop cloths on their leather seats.

I turn to Callie. "Go fetch another throw from the family room. And hurry!"

She scurries off like a frightened rabbit given a reprieve from the jaws of death. I'm not totally confident she's going to return, so it's a relief when she reappears a moment or two later. Swallowing the bile rising up my throat, I take the throw from her outstretched arms and drape it casually over Lincoln's body.

He could never have guessed when he pulled into the garage earlier this evening that his stiffening corpse would be transported out of it only a few hours later.

CHAPTER 21

With Lincoln's body stashed in the car, I turn my attention back to the suicide note. "I'll type something up and you can tell me if it sounds like Lincoln or not," I tell Callie. "It needs to be convincing to his parents more than anyone."

I fall silent for several minutes as I compose an email. I toy with a few variations but, in the end, I keep it short. The more words, the more chance of someone spotting a discrepancy. When I'm done, I read it aloud to Callie.

"I'm sorry for hurting you, darling. I wish with all my heart you hadn't found those photos. I can't live with myself knowing the whole world will soon learn my terrible secrets. I know I'm taking the easy way out but it's better this way."

I blink at Callie expectantly. "What do you think?"

She twists her lips into a petulant pout. "I don't know. It doesn't really sound like him."

"Which part? All of it?"

She frowns at the screen, rereading what I've written. "He would never say 'with all my heart.' To be honest, I'm not sure he would ever admit to what he'd done. He was too selfish for that."

65

"People think differently when they're on the verge of death," I say. "They want to make amends."

She clamps her lips together in a thin line. "At least take out the first sentence about him being sorry for hurting me. It doesn't ring true at all. The only thing he would have been sorry for is that he got caught."

I highlight the sentence and hit delete. "Okay, done. That's good enough. No sense agonizing over it."

"Now what?" Callie asks, hugging her arms around herself.

I glance at the time on my phone. "We'll leave in a couple of hours. We need to make sure there are as few people as possible on the road. You can lie down for a bit, if you want. I'll wake you."

Callie pouts her bottom lip. "I won't be able to sleep."

"Watch TV or something."

She eyes me curiously. "What are you going to do?"

I squeeze the top of my nose between my thumb and forefinger. "Think. I need to comb through our story and make sure we haven't overlooked anything. We're going to have to answer a lot of questions over the next few days."

* * *

Callie is fast asleep when I go into her room to wake her a few hours later.

"It's time," I say, shaking her gently.

She sits bolt upright in bed and gives a jerky nod.

"I need a clean sheet to cover the car seat," I tell her. "I don't want to risk leaving any DNA behind."

Stifling a yawn, she walks over to the closet and pulls out some linens. "Take your pick," she says, thrusting a handful of sheets at me.

"You should wash up," I say. "You've got mascara all over your face and your hair's like a haystack. I'll meet you in the garage. Wear gloves and bring a couple of beanies or baseball caps for us."

66

Five minutes later, the garage door opens, and Callie appears and tosses me a black baseball cap. She walks over to her white Tesla, a ridiculously oversized designer tote slung over her shoulder. Her face is clean, but she still hasn't combed her hair. She's a far cry from the impeccably turned-out woman I first met in Starbucks.

"What?" she asks, narrowing her eyes at me.

"Your hair. If anyone sees you, they're going to think you're high on drugs. We don't want to attract attention."

She gives one of her dramatic sighs. "I don't have a hairbrush on me. Do you have one?"

I roll my eyes. It's hard to believe she doesn't have the entire contents of a beauty salon stashed in her tote. I unzip my purse and hand her my brush. She slides into the driver's seat of her Tesla and makes a lackluster attempt to smooth her hair out in front of the mirror. "There, how's that?" she asks, slapping the hairbrush into my hand.

"Better. At least no one will call the cops on you at a stoplight now."

"Where are we going?" she asks.

"Adobe Canyon Pass." I was mulling over the options in my mind while Callie was sleeping, and I finally settled on the most remote location I know of within an hour's drive of here.

Callie frowns. "I don't know where that is."

"It's a back road into the mountains. It should be deserted at this time of night. Just follow me."

She reaches for the car door to close it.

"Are you sure you're okay to drive?" I ask.

She gives an unconvincing nod and slams the door shut. I have no choice but to trust that she can hold it together. We're going to need her vehicle to get back.

I rap my knuckles on the window and she rolls it down. "One more thing," I say. "Don't turn your lights on until we get to the main road. We can't alert the neighbors."

I drape the sheet carefully over the driver's seat of the Mercedes, then climb in. I won't allow myself to dwell on the fact that there's a dead body behind me that I'm about to illegally dispose of. Everything about this situation is wrong, but telling the truth will put both me and my sister behind bars — a gross miscarriage of justice I can't allow to happen.

Turning on the ignition, I scan the display screen to familiarize myself with the settings. I can't help but admire the luxurious leather interior and elegant craftsmanship of the wood and metal trim. If I could afford a car like this, I would spend every spare minute cruising around in it. Sadly, my current bank balance wouldn't cover filling up the gas tank.

The garage door rolls up and I grip the steering wheel tightly with both hands, bracing myself for the trip ahead. I need to stay focused. I can't be seen driving erratically. And I need to make sure Callie doesn't lose me at a red light. According to my GPS, it's a forty-minute drive to the highest point of Adobe Canyon Pass. It's a treacherous section of road — perfect for what I have in mind.

Once we're clear of the neighborhood, I turn on my headlights and glance in my rear-view mirror to make sure Callie has followed suit. The last thing I need is for her to get pulled over and turn into a blubbering wreck, confessing to everything we've done and are about to do. She seemed so self-assured when we first met — but I'd probably react the same way in her shoes. After all, she's dealing with the shock of her husband's death at her own hands. The problem is, the police will never believe she acted alone — not with my history.

I'm so deep in thought that I barely notice the light at the junction up ahead turning red, and almost slam into the black Ford F-150 in front of me. At the last second, I manage to brake mere inches from the truck's bumper. The car screeches to a halt and Lincoln's blanketed body rolls forward and smacks into the back of my seat. A cold sweat breaks out on my neck. It's almost like he's tapping on my shoulder from the afterlife, giving me one last chance to turn around.

The light turns green and I accelerate, relieved when the truck turns right at the intersection. Hopefully, whoever was driving was too wrapped up in their own world to pay any attention to the vehicle behind them. I'm parched. I lick my dry lips, berating myself for forgetting to bring water. There's a stainless-steel coffee mug in the cupholder, but I don't fancy drinking the dregs of a dead man's cold brew.

I settle in for the drive, but it's a good ten minutes before my heart stops fluttering like a trapped bat inside my chest. I keep imagining what would have happened if I'd crashed into the back of that truck. It's not as if I could have fooled the police into thinking Lincoln died in a minor fender bender.

When I glance in the rear-view mirror again, the Tesla is nowhere in sight.

CHAPTER 22

I slam on the brakes and turn on my blinker, my stomach plummeting faster than a high-speed roller coaster. How did I lose Callie? Or did she chicken out and lose me? Is she parked along the side of the road somewhere, having a full-blown panic attack at the thought of disposing of her husband's body? Surely she hasn't dumped me and ran, leaving me to face the music. *She might be your sister, but she's still a stranger.* My thoughts catapult in a thousand different directions. I can't hang out on the shoulder for long. If a cop comes by, they might stop to make sure I'm okay. I frantically dig in my purse for my phone to call Callie.

"What are you doing?" I blurt out the minute she answers. "Where are you?"

"I forgot to charge my car. I saw there was a charging station, so I thought—"

"Are you out of your mind? We don't have time for this!" I yell into the phone. "You should have checked before we left. How much of a charge do you have?"

"The battery's down to twenty percent. It just chimed at me. Lincoln says I should . . ."

Her voice trails off, as though she's suddenly remembered she can't talk about her husband in the present tense anymore.

"Twenty percent doesn't mean anything to me," I say. "How many miles can you drive on that?"

"Fifty or sixty, I think."

I do a quick calculation in my head. It's too risky. We can't chance getting stuck up on the mountain pass. We might as well have 'guilty' stamped on our foreheads. I grit my teeth in frustration. This would make a great episode of "America's Dumbest Criminals."

"Forget charging your car," I say. "We'll go back and get mine."

"But won't that take just as long?" Callie asks.

"It's less of a risk than stopping for that long to charge your vehicle. Someone might remember seeing your car. Just head straight back to the house. I'll meet you there."

I turn around in a deserted strip mall and begin retracing my route. Despite my efforts to stay calm, anxiety wells up inside me. What if Callie runs out of charge before she gets back to the house? What if she decides to ignore my instructions and charge her vehicle anyway? What if she never shows up? What if she's lying to me about having a low battery and she's really intending to leave me in the lurch?

By the time I pull back into her driveway, my stomach is a seething mass of acid. There's no sign of my sister's vehicle. The thought of having to wait in the Mercedes with Lincoln's body in the pitch black is not an appealing one. I roll to a stop in front of the garage and frantically press the buttons on the rear-view mirror. When the overhead door opens, I pull inside, relief flooding through me at the sight of Callie plugging the wall connecter into her Tesla. I take a moment to compose myself before climbing out. I can't come across like an attack dog. She's fragile enough as it is.

She throws me a fearful look when I walk over to her. "I'm sorry," she says. "My mind was a muddle. I didn't think about checking the charge before we took off."

"It's all right. We still have plenty of time. Do you want to drive the Mercedes or my car?"

"Um, yours, I guess."

It's clear by the look on Callie's face that the thought of driving my clunker is only marginally more appealing than driving around with her husband's dead body. I pull the key from my pocket and hand it to her. She gawps at it like it's a foreign object.

I can't resist a smirk. "It's a 1999. No push-button starts back then. And don't forget, no headlights until we're out of the neighborhood."

I climb inside Lincoln's Mercedes, then slowly back out of the garage and into the driveway.

As I wait for Callie to pull up behind me, a light turns off in the house next door.

CHAPTER 23

I can't think about anything else as I drive but the light switching off next door. Was Callie's neighbor watching us? Was it Lincoln's lover, Vanessa? Or Doug, the jealous husband? Best case scenario, they didn't see anything. But if they did spot us arriving back at the house and leaving again a few minutes later, it would strike them as unusual — something they would be likely to remember if questioned. I groan inwardly. There's no use agonizing over the possibilities. There's nothing I can do about it now, other than hope for the best and prepare for the worst. I won't mention it to Callie. It will only freak her out.

I keep a close eye on my rear-view mirror as I drive. I can't lose her again. My biggest fear is that my 1999 Camry will choose this time to start spewing smoke like a dragon. It wouldn't be the first time, and it certainly won't be the last. My sister has likely never driven a clunker in her life, so she won't recognize the signs and pull over before it's too late. Knowing my luck, she'll be stuck in the middle of the road blocking traffic, drawing unwanted attention to herself. I could call her and warn her that the engine sometimes overheats, but it might just make her more nervous behind the wheel.

The drive seems to take forever, and I find myself tentatively sniffing the air as though Lincoln's body is already beginning to smell. I can't tell if it's my overactive imagination or if that's a real possibility so soon after death. All I know is that the sooner we dispose of him, the better.

At last, I turn onto Adobe Canyon Pass and begin winding my way through the pitch-black mountains. The road continues for another mile or two and dead-ends at a hiking trail. No one will be up here at this time of night. Even so, we're going to need to make this quick. I can't take the risk of some random car showing up in the middle of our attempt to ditch a body.

I slow down and pull over to the shoulder on a dangerous switchback. The embankment drops off a couple of hundred feet into the forest below — more than enough of a plunge to kill a person and hopefully enough to conceal the fact that they were already dead.

Callie pulls up behind me and I wait for her to get out. When she doesn't emerge, I leave the Mercedes engine running and walk over to her. "What are you doing?"

Her gaze flickers in my direction. "Can't I just wait here?"

"Are you kidding me? I need your help. Hurry up! We have to make this quick, and we don't have time for hysterics."

Reluctantly, she clambers out, shivering in the cold night air.

"Help me get him into the driver's seat," I say, turning back to the Mercedes. I open the back door and take a calming breath before tossing the throw onto the ground. I undo the rope, and the blanket falls open, revealing Lincoln's body.

Behind me, Callie moans. My first inclination is to snap at her, but I remind myself that however despicable he was, Lincoln was still her husband.

"Grab his feet," I say, figuring it will be less traumatic for her than having to look at his face. I jog around to the other side of the car and climb into the back seat, then push his body towards the door. It proves easier getting him out than into the driver's seat. His body is already beginning to stiffen, and we struggle for what seems like forever to wedge him behind the steering wheel. I buckle him in, then maneuver myself into position to release the parking brake, trying not to think about the fact that I'm pressing up against Lincoln's dead body.

"Now what?" Callie asks when I slam the car door shut.

She pulls her hair back from her face with trembling fingers, the look of horror forming on her face telling me she already knows the answer.

I steel myself as I walk around to the back of the car. "Now we push."

CHAPTER 24

Back at Callie's house, we sit in the dark at the kitchen table, chugging water as though it might wash away our heinous act.

"I should go," I say at length. "I have to work tomorrow."

"Don't go," Callie begs. "You can sleep here. I don't want to be alone."

I shake my head. "It's better if my car isn't spotted here in the morning. Anything unusual might come to the attention of the police. We need to carry on with our usual routines. Go to the gym tomorrow at the same time you always go."

Callie frowns. "But won't it look suspicious if I don't report Lincoln missing?"

"Not right away." I raise a contemptuous eyebrow. "He was having an affair, remember? Wait at least twenty-four hours. Tell the police it's not unusual for him to be gone for days on end. Stick as close to the truth as possible. You can tell them you argued about his cheating, but you don't recall exactly what time he left the house."

"What about the suicide note?"

"Leave it for the police to find." I sling my purse over my shoulder and get to my feet. "We'll talk again tomorrow. Don't text me. We only ever discuss this in person. Especially once the body has been discovered. The police could be tapping your line, for all you know."

Callie's hand flutters to her neck, terror streaking through her eyes. Once again, I'm second-guessing her ability to see this through. But what choice do I have other than to trust her now that I'm in this deep?

***

My heart lurches in my chest when my alarm goes off a couple of hours later. I sit bolt upright in bed, trying to remember what day of the week it is and where I am. And then it all comes rushing back. I drop my head into my hands and swallow back a guttural sob. What have I done? I'm crying for myself but also for my sister, who will have to live with the haunting memory of everything she did last night, not to mention the guilt. I can't help but picture Brad Halstead, the man I left chained to his bed until he takes his last breath. As awful as it is to admit, it would have been better for both of us if he'd died. I never intended to punish him like I did. He wasn't the monster who assaulted Emma and drove her to an early grave, but he bore the brunt of my rage that day.

With a weary sigh, I stumble out of bed and into the shower. I can't undo the past. I have to stay focused and do exactly what I told Callie to do — act normal and perform my duties as usual. Easier said than done with a boss like Jenna. Nothing escapes her notice.

I greet her with an over-the-top smile that has her antenna up immediately.

"Okay, what's wrong?" she demands, placing a hand on her hip. "And don't tell me nothing. You're only ever this chipper when you're trying to hide something from me."

I hang my purse on a hook, avoiding her gaze for as long as possible. "I'm . . . uh . . . not sleeping the best. The people next door have been playing their music at all hours of the night."

Jenna cocks an eyebrow at me. "I thought you told me you don't hear a thing once you put your earplugs in."

"One of them must have fallen out. The music woke me up and I couldn't get back to sleep." I'm not sure why I'm squirming about telling my boss such a banal lie when I've just helped my sister illegally dispose of her husband's body. Thankfully, Jenna doesn't probe any further.

The morning gets underway, and the flow of customers keeps us occupied for several hours. When there's finally a lull, Jenna pulls me aside. "Forgive me, Piper, but I have to ask you this." Her brow furrows, and dread mounts inside me. She can't possibly know what I've done, but it's hard to keep my irrational thoughts at bay. She's like an intuitive mother on steroids.

"Are you drinking again?" she asks.

My mouth falls open. "What? No! Of course not."

The hard lines on Jenna's face relax. "I'm relieved to hear that. You haven't been yourself this past couple of days and I'm worried about you. I know you're under a lot of stress with your landlord raising the rent, but like I've told you before, I won't see you out on the street. You can always bunk on my couch."

"Thanks, Jenna. I appreciate that."

She wipes her hands on a towel, still scrutinizing me. "That's not it, is it? There's something else bothering you. You were stressed the other day when you took off early for lunch. Did you have a doctor's appointment? Are you sick or something?"

I blow out a heavy breath. I have to tell her about Callie. She'll find out sooner or later anyway. "I discovered my biological sister on myancestry.com. That's who I met up with the other day."

"Piper, that's fantastic news!" Jenna grips me by my arms. "Why the long face? Does she not want a relationship with you?"

"It's not that. I mean, she was a little wary of me at first. It's complicated."

Jenna nods thoughtfully. "You're strangers. You need to give it time."

"She's going through a lot right now," I explain. "I'm trying to support her as best I can. Her husband's having an affair and her stepdaughter's missing."

"Missing?" Jenna echoes. "How old is she?"

"Sixteen."

Jenna rubs a hand over her brow. "She's not that girl on the news, is she? What's her name — the Bramston girl?"

I nod. "Athena Bramston. That's her."

Jenna glances over at the door as the bell jangles. She leans into me, lowering her voice. "Be careful of getting involved with the Bramstons. They're not a family you want to cross."

CHAPTER 25

Jenna's warning hangs with me on the drive home after work. When I pressed her, she was vague about the details, but she mentioned that friends of hers had had business dealings with the Bramstons in the past. They learned the hard way that rich and powerful people always get what they want in the end. It echoes what Callie said about Lincoln's family.

Marco calls me as I'm parking my car on the street outside my apartment. My pulse thunders in my ears. He would never approve of what I've done. I almost let his call go to voicemail, but I know he'll keep calling until I answer. He tried to reach me yesterday too, but I've been avoiding him. It's hard to act like everything's normal when it's anything but. With a resigned sigh, I accept the call. "Hey Marco!"

"Hey! I picked up pizza," he says. "Can I bring some around?"

"I told you before, you don't have to worry about me not eating."

"Somebody has to. I know you're skimping on meals to pay the rent."

I scrunch my eyes shut. He's not wrong. I've been putting off going to the grocery store for longer than usual. There's nothing in the house to eat other than a loaf of bread and possibly some sliced cheese that's starting to go moldy around the edges. The thought of a hot juicy pizza has me salivating. "Fine. Come on over."

I dash around inside the apartment, scooping up a dirty coffee mug, a pile of unopened mail, and the laundry I dumped on the couch several days ago. By the time I'm done picking up, the tiny, 400-square-foot space with fraying sludge-colored carpet, yellowing net curtains, and rickety furniture only looks marginally better. It's why we almost always go to Marco's place to eat or hang out.

There's a knock on the door, and I peer through the peep-hole to make sure it's him before letting him in. He sweeps an appraising gaze around as he places a pizza, two sodas, and a wad of napkins on the counter. "I can't believe your landlord's raising the rent on this dump. He should be offering a discount."

"No kidding. The heater went out again this week. I've been sleeping under every blanket I own, and I still had to wear my coat to bed to keep from freezing."

Marco frowns. "I might have a lead on an apartment for you. A colleague at work said his sister's looking for someone. Her roommate's getting married and moving out at the end of the month."

"How much is the rent?"

"Not sure. I'll find out." He flips open the pizza box lid and spins it around to face me. "Half pepperoni, half BBQ chicken. Just the way you like it."

"Yum." I reach for a slice and nibble on it.

Marco folds a whole slice in half, devours it in a couple of bites, then wipes his mouth. "How's everything going with Callie? I take it that's why you've been ignoring me — too busy with your shiny new sister to keep up with old friends?"

He grins across at me as he reaches for another slice of pizza.

I try to swallow the cheese at the back of my throat and end up choking on it. Marco leans over and thumps me on the back. "You okay?"

81

I nod, my eyes streaming.

"Something I said?" he quips.

I pull the tab on my Diet Coke and take a long draft, before launching into a heavily edited version of events. "I'm sorry I've been preoccupied lately. My sister's in a difficult spot. She found out her husband's been cheating on her. What's worse is that her stepdaughter is missing. I don't watch the news, but supposedly, they've been covering the story. My boss knew about it."

Marco frowns. "I think I caught something about a missing local girl on the TV a few days back. Do the police have any leads?"

"They're handling her as a runaway. She disappeared from her house during the night."

He leans back in his chair. "Wow! Sorry to hear that. I thought your sister was just being a jerk to you, but it does sound like she has a lot going on."

"She's not as tough as she came across initially. She's shattered by Lincoln's betrayal. She says it's not the first time he's messed around behind her back."

"Why doesn't she divorce him?"

"She desperately wants to, but his family's wealthy and well-connected. She has to be strategic about it."

I jump when the doorbell rings.

Marco draws his brows together. "Are you expecting someone?"

I shake my head as I get to my feet. "No, but it might be Callie."

"Check before you open the door," Marco calls after me. "Too many psychos living in this complex."

I look through the peephole and freeze when I see who's on the other side.

CHAPTER 26

I try to steady my breathing, but despite my best efforts, it comes in short, staccato stabs of guilt. What are the police doing outside my door? This can't be good. For once, I wish I had a stash of outstanding parking tickets — anything pedestrian that could explain the police presence on the other side of my apartment door. My mind jumps to the worst-case scenario — Callie has caved and confessed to what she did. She must have implicated me in the process — it would be hard not to. The police would know, to look at her, she must have had help moving her husband's body.

The doorbell rings again and I reach for the handle and wrench it open. I stare blankly at the two uniformed officers. "Can I help you?"

The shorter of the two steps forward, a deadpan expression on his face. "I'm Detective Altman and this is my partner, Officer Marlow. Are you Piper Madden?"

My heartbeat quickens. Maybe I've got this all wrong and Callie hasn't sold me out after all. The police could be here to break some awful news to me. What if Callie couldn't live with what she did and harmed herself? My throat feels like it's closing over.

I flinch when Marco suddenly appears at my side. He glances at the two officers, then back at me. "Is everything all right, Piper?"

I tug nervously at the sleeves on my hoodie. "I'm . . . not sure."

"Can we come in for a few minutes?" Detective Altman asks.

I give a jerky nod. Marco grabs me by the elbow and steers me to the couch as though he's afraid I'm about to collapse.

"Do you want some water?" he asks.

I nod, suddenly nauseated at the lingering smell of pizza in the room. It's mingling in my mind with the odor of Lincoln's decomposing body.

I gulp down most of the water Marco hands me, then turn to the officers, bracing myself for what it is they're here to tell me.

Altman clears his throat. "I'm sorry to have to inform you that your brother-in-law's body was discovered in his car by hikers early this morning."

The gasp that escapes my lips isn't forced. I'm shocked to hear they found his body so soon. I estimated Callie and I would have several days to fine tune our story, and several days of decomposition to corroborate it. My hand shakes as I set down my glass. "My . . . sister?"

What I really want to ask is if the police have broken the news to Callie yet, but Altman misunderstands my question.

"She's okay," he says. "Her husband was the only occupant in the vehicle."

Marco slides an arm around my shoulders and pulls me close. I don't react, even though I register the fact that it's not something he's ever done before.

"So, it was a car accident?" I ask, in a breathy tone.

Altman's eyebrows knot together. "It's too early to determine that. What I can tell you is that his vehicle went off the road on Adobe Canyon Pass last night."

The ball of fear in my belly grows as I wait for him to continue. How much has Callie told him? Everything? Nothing? Did she sit there and feign shock and bewilderment as I'm attempting to do?

"Has her sister been informed?" Marco interjects, unwittingly sparing me the stress of asking the question. I already have all the answers the police are seeking. I only hope my expression doesn't give that away.

"Yes," Altman confirms. "Her in-laws are with her right now. She was very distraught, as you might imagine."

A flicker of unease goes through me when I think of Jenna's words. *They're not a family you want to cross.* It's naive to think the Bramstons will accept their son's suicide without contesting it.

"Miss Madden," Detective Altman prompts, reclaiming my attention, "a neighbor reported seeing your vehicle at your sister's residence late last night."

Marco's hand on my shoulder tenses.

"M-my car?" My voice spirals upward despite my attempt to sound unfazed. Did the neighbors see us leave too? My heart pounds mercilessly in my chest. "Yes, I was there. I've been spending a lot of time with my sister over the past few days. We only just found each other on myancestry.com."

Altman gives a fleeting smile. "She mentioned you were adopted." He clears his throat. "I understand the security cameras at the house are not working. Do you know what time Lincoln left the residence last night?"

I frown in faux concentration. *The same time I did.*

85

CHAPTER 27

I squeeze my fingers in my lap as I weigh my response. Is Altman testing me? Maybe he already knows the answer to his question, and he's waiting for me to dig a hole and incriminate myself. I can't answer any more of his questions until I know what Callie has told him. Did she tell him she found the stalking photos? Does he know about Lincoln's affair? Or that he assaulted me? If our stories don't line up, Altman will attack like a rabid dog.

"Are you okay?" Marco whispers in my ear.

"It's just so . . . unbelievable." I throw Altman a piteous look. "I really need to be with my sister right now."

"I understand, but it's important for us to establish a timeline." He blinks expectantly at me, triggering a panicked response.

"I'm, uh . . . not sure when Lincoln left. He didn't tell us he was leaving." I knit my brows together. "He and Callie are going through a bit of a rough patch—" I frown as I catch what I'm saying. "Were."

Altman tilts his head toward me. "Are you talking about the fact that Lincoln's daughter is missing?"

"That didn't help. But their relationship has been rocky for some time now. Callie told me Lincoln was having an affair — she thinks with one of their neighbors. It's not the first time he's cheated on her."

"Did your sister and her husband argue last night?"

"Yes. She confronted him about his cheating. He stormed out afterward."

"What time was that at?"

I squirm in my seat. "I think around eleven. I stayed on for a few hours after that."

Altman makes some notes, then eyes me shrewdly. "What did you and your sister talk about that late into the night?"

I give a non-committal shrug. "Nothing in particular. We're making up for lost time."

"Your sister must have been upset after the argument. Did you discuss her relationship with her husband?"

The fluttering in my chest increases. "A little. I tried to be supportive of her."

"Did she ever talk about wanting to get out of the relationship?"

I snatch a breath. "You mean . . . divorce?"

A small smile curls at the corner of Altman's lips. "What else?"

My brain feels like it's stalling. I wish this interview would end before I blow it. I desperately need to talk to Callie. "I . . . told her she should leave him."

"What was her response?"

I shrug. "Nothing. I'm not exactly her confidante. We don't know each other all that well yet."

Detective Altman flicks through his notebook as though searching for something, then suddenly snaps it shut. "I think that's all the information I need for now. Thank you for your time, Miss Madden. I'll be in touch if I have any more questions."

I half rise out of my seat, then sink back down, my legs wobbling beneath me.

Marco gives my shoulder a reassuring squeeze. "I'll see them out."

I nod mutely, shivering to myself as I watch Altman and his cohort troop out of the apartment. I need to call Callie right away and find out what she told them. Not the truth, evidently, or the cops would have arrested me on the spot. She doesn't want to go to prison either.

I struggle to my feet when Marco returns to the kitchen. "I need to go see Callie."

He frowns. "Are you sure that's a good idea?"

"I'm her sister. Her husband just died. It's the least I can do." I pull out my phone and dial her number. It goes straight to voicemail. I hang up and try again. This time she answers. "They found him!" she sobs into the phone. "The police were here asking all sorts of questions."

"Don't say anything more. I'm coming over right now. Are your in-laws still there?"

"No. They left already. They wanted to start calling people. What did you tell—"

"Not on the phone. We'll talk when I get there." My hands shake as I slip my phone into the back pocket of my jeans.

"I'll drive you," Marco says. "You're in no fit state to get behind the wheel."

"I'll be fine."

"I'm not taking no for an answer. You're in shock, Piper."

"I don't think Callie's going to want you there."

"I'll go grab some coffee and come back and pick you up when you're done."

I shrug, too weary to argue the point any further. Besides, I really could use a ride. Altman's visit has shaken me to the core. It's only now hitting me what I've done, and I'm suffocating under the weight of guilt.

I don't want to end up plunging into a ravine in the dark of night like Lincoln, but I'm scared of what I might do if I'm left alone.

CHAPTER 28

True to his word, Marco drops me off at Callie's house and drives off the minute she answers the door. I'd rather the two of them don't cross paths until I've had a chance to talk with Callie and made sure she hasn't botched the version of events we agreed to stick to.

We walk silently to the kitchen, contemplating our next move. A shiver skitters across my shoulders. The house I was coveting only a couple of days earlier has taken on the air of a mausoleum.

"Do you want something to drink?" Callie asks, leaning back against the counter.

I shake my head and glance nervously around the space. "Did the police search the house?"

"They asked if they could look around." Her eyes widen. "Is that bad? I didn't pay much attention to what they were doing."

"What do you mean you didn't pay much attention?" I ask impatiently. "Did they find the suicide note?"

Callie traces her fingers lightly over her forehead. "If they did, they didn't mention it. I don't think they did an extensive search."

89

My stomach knots. She should have made them get a warrant. Now we have no idea what the police saw, or photographed, or bagged as evidence. I grab her by the arm. "Let's talk outside on the back patio."

Callie pouts her lip. "Why? It's cold out there."

Ignoring her, I open the sliding French doors and take a seat on a luxurious patio chair. Callie digs some blankets out from a wicker basket and tosses me one.

"I don't understand why we have to sit out here," she complains, pulling a blanket around her shoulders.

"The police might have bugged your house. What did you tell Altman?"

"Exactly what we agreed on — Lincoln walked out of the house and didn't tell me where he was going." She scowls. "Nothing unusual in that."

I twist a strand of hair distractedly around my finger. "Do you think the police believed you?"

"Why wouldn't they?"

I throw her a withering look. I can think of a dozen reasons why they might be skeptical.

"Did they ask about the security cameras?" I ask.

Callie beams at me like she's angling for an "A" on a school project. "Of course. I told them they weren't working, and that Lincoln kept promising to have someone from Secure First come out and take a look, but they never called him back and he never followed up."

I let out a groan. "Way too much information. You should have just told the cops the cameras weren't working and left it at that. If Altman calls Secure First, which he will, he'll find out pretty quickly that Lincoln never contacted them."

Callie shrugs. "I'll say he often lied to me about stuff. He was a jerk."

I shoot her a look of alarm. "Don't say it with such disdain. If it's obvious you despised him, you'll arouse suspicion."

A rustling sound at the side of the house catches my attention. I freeze and put a finger to my lips. "Someone's out here," I whisper.

Callie shivers, gripping her blanket tighter as she darts frantic glances around the gloomy shapes and shadows surrounding the expansive lawn.

"Let's go back inside," I mutter, scrambling to my feet. My heart hammers out a frenetic rhythm in my chest. I have a horrible feeling Callie's neighbors have been eavesdropping on our conversation. They must have been curious about what was happening with the cars coming and going. My skin crawls at the thought of someone overhearing us. I frantically run back through what I discussed with Callie. Did we say anything incriminating? My heart sinks when snatches of conversation come back to me. I only hope it was a dog or something outside, and not Vanessa or Doug.

Back in the kitchen, I scoot my chair closer to Callie's. "How did Lincoln's parents take the news?" I ask.

"How do you think? Not well. They chewed the cops out for not having all the answers to their questions, and they threatened them with legal action if they botch the investigation."

"Ssh! Keep your voice down! What do you mean by investigation?"

"They have to determine what happened, don't they? They're looking for any signs that Lincoln tried to brake or swerve to avoid another vehicle."

Sweat beads along my forehead. "We can't have them wasting time going down that path. You need to call Detective Altman and tell him you found a suicide note, and surveillance photos of women."

Callie blinks at me wide-eyed. "When?"

"Now!" I pull out my phone and shoot Marco a quick text letting him know I'm done. "I can't be here when Altman gets here," I say, getting to my feet.

A stricken look crosses Callie's face. "Why not?"

"It would look odd. I was here the night Lincoln died, and now I just happen to be here again when you discover the suicide note."

My phone beeps with an incoming message from Marco letting me know he's outside. He can't have been too far away when I texted.

"What are you waiting for?" I say to Callie.

With an air of trepidation, she picks up her phone and punches in the number. I listen in on the conversation, punctuated by Callie's crocodile tears as she describes finding a heart-wrenching email in Lincoln's draft folder, and some suspicious photos.

I give an approving nod when she hangs up. "Call me once Altman leaves and let me know how it goes."

Callie picks at the sleeve of her designer sweater. "Do you really think we're going to get away with this?"

"Yes," I say, leaning over to hug her slim frame. "I do. If you need to talk, don't call me. You know where to find me. Come by any time, day or night."

I hurry out of the house and down the front steps to where Marco is parked, the engine running.

"That was quick," I say, reaching for my seatbelt. "I texted you, and two minutes later, you were here."

He stares straight ahead without saying a word.

"Marco, is everything all right?" I ask, peering over at him.

He turns to me slowly, his eyes reflective pools of sadness. "I overheard you talking out back. Piper, what did you do?"

CHAPTER 29

My blood runs cold at Marco's question. Was that him I heard moving around in the bushes at the side of the house? I cut him an indignant glare. "Were you spying on us?"

"Not intentionally. I was sitting in the car with the window rolled down, and I heard voices. I didn't know you were sitting outside — I thought someone was creeping around the house. I was worried about you, so I went to check it out."

My whole body is breaking out in a cold sweat. I can't involve Marco in this. He was gracious enough not to hold my past against me, but this is different. Illegally disposing of a body is enough to put me back behind bars. If I tell Marco what I've done, I'll be putting him in a terrible position. He'll be compelled to talk if the police question him.

"You had no right to trespass," I say, choking out the words. It's hard to sound reproving when my voice is shaking.

"I know you're scared, Piper."

He reaches for my hand, but I snatch it away. "You don't know anything."

He exhales loudly as he puts the car in gear and pulls out of the driveway. "You don't have to tell me what's going on if

93

you don't want to. But I'm here for you if you need someone to talk to."

"I was just warning Callie not to talk herself into a trap," I huff. "They're investigating her husband's death. You know how cops can be."

Marco says nothing, but he looks unconvinced. We barely talk for the remainder of the journey, limiting our exchanges to banal comments about work and our next AA meeting.

Marco doesn't get out of the car when he drops me off at my apartment complex. He normally walks me in to make sure I get safely past my questionable neighbors. I can't blame him for being upset with me. He knows I lied to him.

Inside my apartment, I pace back and forth across the cramped space like a caged animal. In my mind, I sift through the events of the past twenty-four hours, searching for discrepancies and weaknesses in our story. Anything has the potential to expose us, but it's too late now to redo any of the actions we've taken. I need to stop obsessing over it or I'll fall apart. What's done is done. I must stay strong for Callie's sake.

I sleep fitfully and end up texting Jenna in the early hours to let her know about Lincoln's "accident" and that I'm running late for work. When I finally roll in, she raises a subtle brow at the heavy bags beneath my eyes but doesn't comment on my haggard appearance. Instead, she envelops me in one of her all-consuming hugs. "I'm so sorry, honey. What a horrible thing to happen."

Somehow, I get through work in a stupor. When I clock out, I drive straight to Callie's house. She's been bombarding me with texts all day. As I clamber out of my car in her driveway, I notice the next-door neighbors standing on their front steps, eyes glued on me. I feel like I'm under a microscope, my every move being examined. I force a stiff smile and wave woodenly at them. Ignoring my gesture, they turn their backs and disappear inside their mansion. I'm not sure what message they're trying to convey. Maybe they simply resent me showing up in their neighborhood in a beat-up Camry. Or they could have seen that Camry driving off in the middle of the night and returning a couple of hours later.

Acid slithers up my throat as I consider the possibilities. What if they suspect me of something nefarious? The police must have talked to them by now. I'm terrified of what they might have said. At least they didn't overhear my conversation with Callie in the backyard. I can trust Marco to keep his mouth shut, no matter how disappointed he is in me.

"Your neighbors were giving me the stink-eye," I comment to Callie as I follow her into the kitchen.

"I'm not surprised. I told Altman I suspected Lincoln was having an affair with Vanessa. He must have talked to them. I'm sure she denied it." She picks at her fingernails. "Do you think they saw something?"

I give a small shrug as I sink down in a kitchen chair. "Someone reported seeing my car parked outside your house, but I don't know if they saw us leave together."

Callie fidgets with her hair. "Want some coffee?"

"No thanks. And neither do you. I can tell you're already wired." I gesture impatiently to the chair next to me. "Sit down. How did things go with Altman?"

"Good." Callie blinks at me, sucking her bottom lip. "I think."

"What do you mean you *think*?" I reply, trying to keep the irritation out of my voice.

"I don't know. He was hard to read. He didn't seem surprised or shocked about the suicide note. He didn't really react."

"That's because he's trained not to. What did he say?"

"He asked me when I discovered it. I told him it was right before I called him. I was going through Lincoln's emails to see if there was anything important that needed to be taken care of. The police took the computer with them."

"That's good," I say. "Altman will be able to see that the email was written before Lincoln left the house that night. It will bolster our story. What did he say about the photos?"

Callie drops her gaze, twisting her hands in her lap. "I don't have them anymore."

CHAPTER 30

"What do you mean you don't have the photos? What did you do with them?"

"I showed them to Lincoln's mother. I think she took them with her when she left."

I slap my head, half rising out of my seat. "How could you have let her get her hands on them? She won't turn them over to the police. She'll probably destroy them to protect her son's reputation."

"I . . . I wasn't thinking straight. Eleanor blew in here like a tornado accusing me of being the source of all Lincoln's problems. I told her she had it all backwards — that he was abusive and that he'd cheated on me multiple times. I showed her the pictures to prove to her what her son was really like. I was hoping she would take my side, for once. But she acted like the photos meant nothing — told me I was a rotten wife and a liar. She was screaming at me. I couldn't take it anymore. I burst out crying and ran to the bathroom and locked the door. When I came back out, she and Theo were gone. I didn't notice the photos were missing until several hours later."

I let out a frustrated groan. "At least I managed to snap some pictures. They're not as good as the originals but they have to be worth something."

"I'm scared, Piper," Callie says in a raspy whisper. "You don't know what that family's capable of."

"You can't let them get in your head. You're going to need to muster your fighting spirit to see this through. Of course they don't want their precious son's reputation sullied. How did Altman react when you told him you suspected Vanessa and Lincoln were having an affair?"

"He asked me if I had any evidence. I told him Lincoln has a track record of cheating and that I'd caught him having secret conversations with Vanessa. I mentioned the photos too. He didn't seem impressed."

"Is he going to question Vanessa at least?"

"He said he would interview all the neighbors as a matter of course. I think he's already been over to see them." She throws me a harried look. "Should we be concerned?"

"No. We would have been arrested by now if Vanessa or Doug had seen anything. What else did you and Altman talk about?"

"I asked him if there was any indication that Lincoln had tried to brake and he said no — based on the trajectory, the car was going very slowly at the time. They're waiting on the autopsy results to find out if Lincoln had alcohol or drugs in his system."

I give a satisfied nod. "All standard stuff."

I flinch at the sound of a car peeling into the gravel courtyard. I lock eyes with Callie. "Are you expecting someone?"

She shakes her head. "It's probably just a delivery. They always drive too fast and churn up the gravel."

I wait for the doorbell to chime but instead I hear the front door opening.

Callie's eyes shimmer with fear. Before she can utter another word, a woman in a powder-gray pantsuit, pearls, and kitten heels glides into the kitchen. Her frosty blue eyes sweep up and down me in one efficient brush stroke. "You must be the *sister.*"

"Um, yes. I'm Piper Madden. And you must be Eleanor Bramston." It would be polite to say "I'm sorry for your loss," but the words get stuck in my throat.

She whisks an imaginary crumb from the counter and sets down her designer clutch before turning back to me. "I assume you have proof of this lineage?"

"I have paperwork from—"

"Never mind all that," she cuts in, flapping a hand at me. "I can see from your unfortunate features that you're related."

I dart a glance in Callie's direction. She has a wounded expression on her face, but a hint of anger glitters in her eyes.

Eleanor Bramston takes a seat at the table between us and pins her gaze on Callie. "Theo's in the car finishing up an important call. I'll take a coffee, black, while we're waiting."

I try not to squirm under Eleanor's penetrating stare as Callie busies herself at the coffee maker.

"You must have been delighted when you discovered your sister had married into a wealthy family," Eleanor says, an unpleasant grin on her face.

I force myself to hold her gaze. "I expect you were equally thrilled for your daughter-in-law when she found out she had a blood relative."

Eleanor reaches for the cup Callie sets in front of her and takes a sip, studying me over the rim. "I understand you were here the night my son died."

"Yes. I've been with my sister almost every day since we found each other online."

"Indeed." Eleanor sets her cup back in the saucer and tents her fingers in front of her while resting her elbows on the table. "Quite the coincidence that right after my granddaughter goes missing, you show up, and then my son dies."

"Unfortunate timing, for sure," I reply. Outwardly I'm trying to maintain my composure but inwardly I'm a quivering wreck.

I turn my head at the sound of the front door opening again. To my surprise, two men walk into the room. The older one, a stout man with a thatch of gray hair, eyes me coldly, before walking over to Callie and giving her a perfunctory hug.

"My husband, Theo," Eleanor says, gesturing to him. She turns to the younger man. "And this is Henry Faulkner, a private investigator who's going to get to the bottom of what really happened to our son."

"Me and" Theo… Altman's a go-getter, that. He sure is discerning and… And busy. Henry Faulkner's a private investigator who's going to get to the bottom blood—

CHAPTER 31

My mouth drops open. I turn to Henry Faulkner and do a quick assessment in my mind. He's young, early thirties, likely inexperienced, but his eyes are shrewd and penetrating. Not to be underestimated. He's well-dressed for a PI, sporting an expensive-looking, crisp white shirt and saddle-brown sports coat. The Bramstons aren't short on money, so I'm guessing Henry is one of the best PIs available for hire.

"I retained Henry to help us find Athena, given the incompetence of the police," Theo says. "He'll be looking into Lincoln's death now too."

Henry hitches his lips into a disarming smile as he hands me his card. "I look forward to your cooperation, Piper."

Eleanor takes another sip of coffee, a satisfied expression on her face as she gauges my reaction. Callie never mentioned that her mother-in-law had hired a PI to look for Athena. It's good to know she cares that much. Despite her immaculately made-up face, she hasn't been able to disguise the heavy bags beneath her eyes. First her only grandchild goes missing and now her son is dead. Whatever inadequacies she perceives Altman to possess, I have no doubt Henry Faulkner is being handsomely compensated to make up for them. Eleanor will leave no stone unturned in her search for answers in the death of her only child.

"I thought Lincoln committed suicide," I say, trying in vain to stop my jaw from trembling. "Callie told me he wrote her an email apologizing for taking the easy way out."

Eleanor gives a disgusted grunt. "Lincoln would never have committed suicide."

I wrinkle my brow. "But the police told Callie there was no indication he had braked or swerved to avoid another vehicle."

"Which is exactly why we've hired Faulkner," Eleanor snaps. "We can't depend on the police. They're only concerned with wrapping things up as quickly as possible. The detective on the case is useless."

"Eleanor, dear," Theo interrupts, "they're doing the best they can. We can't afford to aggravate them, or they might start shutting us out of the investigation."

Eleanor shoots daggers across the room at her husband. "If Altman is their best, it's no wonder our cities are swarming with criminals."

Theo pinches the bridge of his nose and turns his attention back to his phone.

"Faulkner," Eleanor goes on, "how do you want to handle this? Do you want to interview the girls separately?"

"That won't be necessary," he replies. "At least not for our initial conversation."

Callie and I exchange a loaded look. Surely we're not obligated to talk to him. But it would look suspicious to refuse.

Faulkner pulls out his phone and places it on the table as he takes a seat. "If no one has any objections, I'd like to record this to refer back to later."

"Fine with me," Callie says.

Eleanor raises her expertly penciled eyebrows at me.

I shrug. "Sure," I say. "I assume Henry mostly wants to talk to Callie, but I'm happy to jump in and answer any questions I can."

"I'm interested in what both of you have to say." Henry leans back in his chair and swings one leg over the other as though he hasn't a care in the world. Sweat prickles across the back of my neck. He could prove more dangerous than Altman. He has a vested interest in making his employers happy, and nothing would delight Eleanor Bramston more than to prove her son didn't commit suicide.

"Let's start with you, Callie," Henry says. "I'd like to go over everything that happened that night in the hours prior to Lincoln driving off. What time did he come home from work?"

Callie frowns. "Around seven or so. Piper and I were in the kitchen. We spoke briefly, then Lincoln went into his office and closed the door. We didn't see him for the rest of the evening."

Henry clears his throat, an expression of regret settling over his face. "I apologize for asking a delicate question, but I understand you and Lincoln argued that evening."

I shift a little in my chair. His delivery is flawless. He's charming, slippery as a snake. I only hope he doesn't mesmerize Callie into saying something she shouldn't.

She wets her lips, her eyes flicking briefly in Eleanor's direction. "It's no secret we've been arguing a lot lately. I accused Lincoln of having an affair. He's cheated on me in the past, and all the signs were there again."

Eleanor rolls her eyes. "You can hardly blame the man. He was only welcome in his own home when he was signing checks."

"Are you trying to justify him cheating on his wife?" I cut in.

Henry raises a hand mid-air to stop a retaliatory tirade from Eleanor. She purses her lips and glares at me.

"Eleanor," Henry says, "it's important that everyone gets a chance to tell me what happened in their own words. Piper, I'll get to you in a moment. Until then, I'd appreciate it if both of you would let Callie continue uninterrupted."

I sink back in my chair, avoiding looking in Eleanor's direction. I can't help thinking about the missing surveillance photos. She's probably destroyed them. There's nothing she wouldn't do to protect her son's reputation.

And nothing will stop her digging until she gets to the truth of how he died.

CHAPTER 32

At group that night, my head's on a swivel looking for Marco.
I've saved him a seat, but I'm not sure he's going to want to
sit next to me, if he shows up at all. I desperately need to talk
to him, but, for the first time in years, the session begins with
no sign of him. Anxiety swirls in the pit of my stomach. Is he
deliberately avoiding me, or has something happened? I feel
like I'm breaking out in hives from equal measures of fear and
guilt. I can barely sleep with the weight of everything hanging
over me.

"Surprised you showed up tonight," Marco mutters, startling me as he slides into the seat next to mine. A flash flood
of relief rushes through me. His tone isn't particularly frosty,
but he's not his usual jovial self either. If I had to guess, he's
only halfway thawed out, and deliberately showed up late to
make me sweat a little.

"I need to talk to you," I whisper to him.

He stuffs his hands deep into his pockets and stretches
out his legs in front of him. "If you're going to feed me more
lies, I'm not interested."

At the front of the room, John gets to his feet to open
the meeting, giving me a temporary reprieve. But I won't be

able to fob Marco off indefinitely. I spend the entirety of the session contemplating whether to come clean with him. I'd be putting him in an awful predicament. He'd be torn between going to the police with information about a crime and protecting me from a second prison term. I don't honestly know what I would do if I were in his shoes. Before I know it, the meeting has concluded, and it dawns on me that I have no clue what the topic tonight was.

"Great talk, John," I say, when he shakes my hand afterward and thanks me for coming.

He puckers his brow. "Are you okay, Piper? You seemed a little out of it tonight."

I flash a smile so plastic it feels like my lips are about to crack. "Just tired, that's all. See you next week." I turn and hurry out of the room before he can follow up with any more questions. I wait in the foyer for Marco, and we trudge out to our cars in silence.

"Do you want to grab a coffee or something?" I ask.

He runs a hand over the top of his head. "Let's just sit in my car and you can tell me what it is you have to tell me."

I grimace as I walk around to the passenger side of his car. It's clear that if I don't come clean about what he overheard, our relationship could fritter away. I can't risk losing one of the few relationships that means anything to me.

Marco switches on the engine and cranks up the heat. For a moment or two, I say nothing. I don't know what the right thing is to do anymore. I let out a heavy sigh. "I know you're upset with me for lying to you, but I did it to protect you. And to protect myself from the possibility of losing our friendship. If I told you the truth, I'd be putting you in a terrible position."

He looks away and stares through the windscreen, fingers resting loosely on the bottom of the steering wheel. "We promised each other a long time ago we'd be there for each other no matter what. Give me the chance to prove that to you. I don't know what you've done, but I'm guessing it has something to do with your brother-in-law."

I drop my head, silent tears coursing down my cheeks.

Marco thumps the steering wheel, then turns to me. "I can't stand to see you this cut up. Spit it out, Piper. Did you kill him? Did you run him off the road or something?"

I give a vehement shake of my head. "No! Nothing like that."

"Then what?"

"It . . . was an accident."

Marco stares at me, his brow wrinkled in confusion. "How was it an accident? It was the middle of the night on a remote road. You must have followed him."

"You don't understand."

I pull a tissue from my purse and mop my sodden eyelashes. Then I tell him everything.

CHAPTER 33

"You hate me now, don't you?" I say.

Marco rubs his jaw. "I could never hate you, but I'm not going to lie. You've done something very stupid. This isn't going to be an easy fix."

"I'm not asking you to fix it. This isn't some car battery you can pick up at Walmart and *hey presto!* life is good again."

Marco shoots me an injured look. "What's that supposed to mean?"

I reach over and squeeze his shoulder. "Nothing. I'm sorry. I didn't mean to sound condescending. It's just that I know how you like to fix things. You've always been there for me when I needed something. But this is different. You can't help me this time. The Bramstons have hired a top-notch PI to investigate Lincoln's death. I'm not going to let you go down with me if things go sideways."

Marco looks grim. "And they may very well. You don't know your sister. If the police suspect she had something to do with this, they'll grill her until they break her. Like you said yourself, she's not as strong as you thought she was. She was acting large and in charge when all she had to worry about was her exercise regime and her designer wardrobe. But covering up a murder is out of her league."

"It wasn't murder, it was an accident. And I know she's not equipped to deal with the situation. That's why I'm helping her. She's been abused for years. She doesn't know how to fight for herself. I can't let her go to prison for this. You would do the same thing for me."

"Maybe," he says distractedly.

"Are you going to go to the police?" I ask, holding my breath as I await his reply.

He squares his jaw. "Of course not. But I wish you'd told me this when it happened. That cop came by my house today and asked a bunch of questions."

My skin crawls. "Altman, the one who came by my apartment?"

Marco nods. "Yeah."

I press my nails into the palms of my hands. He can't be as incompetent as the Bramstons made him out to be if he's already homing in on my small circle of friends and acquaintances. I wonder if he's questioned Jenna too. "What did he ask about?"

"He wanted to know all about your relationship with Callie, how long you've known each other, how you found out about each other, what you told me about your sister, how long you've known your niece was missing, that kind of thing."

"What did you tell him?"

"That Lincoln was abusive to your sister. That you couldn't stand to see a woman being bullied by a man and you told her to leave him." He groans and rubs his hands over his face. "Now you know why I wish you'd told me the truth earlier. I'd have been more careful with my words. I was trying to portray you as a concerned sister and instead I've set you up as a potential vigilante suspect."

He turns to me, a drawn look in his eyes. "Don't tell me not to get involved, Piper. Because I am involved now. Thanks to me, you're one step closer to being charged with Lincoln's murder."

CHAPTER 34

"The first thing you need is a good lawyer," Marco says.

I snort in disgust. "I'm not going to hire a lawyer. That will make me look guilty. Besides, the good ones don't accept payment in scones or cupcakes."

Marco throws me a reproving look. "This isn't funny, Piper. You know I'll cover the cost. You could be facing serious prison time if Altman finds out what you've done."

"But he's not going to, is he? The only people who know the truth about what happened that night are you, me, and Callie. She's not going to squeal — she doesn't want to go to prison. And I know you would never betray me."

Marco sets his jaw and starts the engine. "I've got to go. I have an early morning online meeting. Think about my offer. You need to handle this the right way."

I open the car door, an uneasy feeling swirling in the pit of my stomach. I rolled the dice by confessing to Marco — believing he wouldn't turn me in. But what if I'm wrong? What if his conscience won't allow him to keep it under wraps? Our relationship has been strained ever since I lied to him about my conversation with Callie. I had hoped to put things right by coming clean with him, but what if I'm beyond the point of no return? If he doesn't trust me anymore, I can't trust him either.

I plod over to my car, feeling the weight of my deception with every laborious step. Now I have two people to worry about who could inadvertently, or deliberately, change the course of my life, and not for the better. I'm only digging my own grave deeper with every decision I make.

I'm sorely tempted to call Marco on the drive home and try to get some reassurance from him that my secret is safe. But I know him too well. He's his own man and not easily influenced. He needs time to sit with this. If I press him now, I might push him in the opposite direction. I only hope loyalty to our friendship supersedes his conscience in whatever decision he makes.

When I pull into my apartment complex, I'm shocked to see Callie's white Tesla in the parking lot, engine running. My heart skips a beat as myriad possibilities shoot through my head. I hurry over to her car and knock on the window. Her head jerks up from her phone, eyes wide with alarm until she realizes it's me.

She switches off the engine and clambers out, shooting a withering glance around as though weighing up the neighborhood and finding it wanting.

"What's going on?" I ask.

"Let's talk inside," she says, pulling her camel wool coat tighter around her.

I rack my brain trying to remember what state I left the apartment in before heading out to group. I'm pretty sure my things are strewn all over as usual. Other than the occasional visit from Marco, no one ever darkens my door, so I don't see the point in tidying up. I grimace as I lead Callie into the dingy foyer. Hopefully, she doesn't need to use the bathroom — it's always in disarray and in desperate need of cleaning. Not the first impression of my habitat I want to give my glamorous sister.

I put the key in the lock and twist, ramming the door at the same time.

Callie flinches and takes a step back.

"Don't worry. It always sticks," I say with a forced chuckle. "This is my usual method of entry."

Callie follows me inside, her eyes trailing over the clutter piled high on the minuscule kitchen counter.

"Sorry about the mess," I say, hurriedly scooping up a pile of ironing from one end of the couch. "I wasn't expecting company."

She perches on the edge of a seat cushion, examining one of her artificial nails.

"Do you want something to drink?" I ask, dreading her response. The refrigerator is empty, and I'm pretty sure I'm out of coffee. I could drum up a teabag if I poked around a bit, but it's not as if I have honey or a wedge of lemon to accompany it. I don't have any bottled water either, and I doubt Callie would be okay with drinking unfiltered water from my faucet.

"No, thanks," she says, squeezing her hands together and shivering.

"The heater's broken," I say with an apologetic shrug. "My landlord's sending someone out to look at it."

I sink down on the other end of the couch, adjusting my position when I hit a spring. My heart thuds an ominous beat in my chest. I told Callie to come by any time, but I'm pretty sure she wouldn't deign to visit my neighborhood unless she had a really compelling reason. I only hope she's not going to tell me she wants to confess. Not after all the illegal things I've done to help her.

I wait patiently for a moment or two, as she continues to wring her hands despairingly.

"What did you want to talk to me about?" I prompt.

She scrunches her eyes shut and takes a shallow breath before responding. "They have the preliminary autopsy results."

CHAPTER 35

I swallow the lump in my throat. Judging by Callie's fraught expression, this isn't a good thing. Surely the coroner wouldn't be able to tell that Lincoln tumbled down a flight of stairs before plunging into a ravine in his Mercedes. Did the police discover something we overlooked? Were Lincoln's injuries not compatible with a car wreck? My thoughts dart this way and that like manic meteorites inside my head. I need to stay calm and wait for the facts. However this plays out, I have to demonstrate confidence to Callie. It's the only way I'm going to keep her on board long enough to see this thing through to the other side.

"Don't leave me hanging," I say to her.

She sniffs back tears as she brushes the sleeve of her coat over her eyes. "The coroner determined that Lincoln was already dead when the car went into the ravine."

My skin prickles. I take a deep breath and sink back on the couch, trying to curb the sense of dread enveloping me. "Well, we already knew that, so no surprise there."

"How can you be so blasé about it!" Callie wails. "They're going to do a full-blown investigation now. And fancy-pants PI Henry is going to be snooping around too. I had no idea Theo and Eleanor had hired him to search for Athena."

I raise my hands in front of me in a calming gesture. "Take it easy, Callie. This doesn't change anything. We stick to our story. Lincoln could have had a medical emergency — a stroke or something. Maybe he blacked out at the wheel."

"Stop! Please, stop!" Callie pleads. "None of that's going to fly. Eleanor showed me the autopsy report. They know Lincoln had been dead for several hours before the Mercedes crashed. They can tell from the computer in the car the exact time the engine quit." She rubs a hand over her face. "They have to know he was murdered — there's no other explanation."

"They don't know anything," I assure her. "They can speculate all they want, but they can't link us to his death. We have to make sure they look for a suspect elsewhere. A man like Lincoln must have made plenty of enemies. You need to remind them about the surveillance photos. If Lincoln assaulted any of those women, they would have a motive to get revenge. A boyfriend or a husband could have come after him."

"Do you still have copies of those photos?" Callie asks.

I fish my phone from my pocket. "I'll forward them to you right now."

She studies them dubiously. "Can a photo of a photo even be considered evidence?"

"I don't know, but it paints a picture of Lincoln and that's what's important. He was a cheater, a liar, and an abuser. And men like that make enemies. If the police think he was murdered, our job is to make sure they have suspects with motives, other than us."

"I'm more worried about that PI than Detective Altman," Callie says, twisting her wedding ring around on her finger. "I looked him up online. He's an ex-police officer and he has a degree in psychology."

"Then we need to give him something to go after. He's already been working on locating Athena. We suggest a link between her disappearance and Lincoln's murder. It could have had something to do with a shady business deal. Wealthy families always have lots of secrets."

113

"But won't it look like we're trying to deflect if we suggest that to Henry?"

"It would have to be an anonymous tip."

Callie frowns. "How are we going to pull that off? We'd have to disguise our voices."

I try not to roll my eyes at her naivety. "We're not going to call Henry. We'll send him an anonymous email. I know just the person to help us."

CHAPTER 36

After Callie left, I tried calling Marco, but he didn't pick up, so I had to resort to sending him a text, more or less begging for his help. I didn't elaborate on exactly what kind of help I need — he won't be thrilled to learn it's the illegal kind. But like he said, he's involved now. This will be a good test to determine if he's with me or full of hot air.

I leave my phone on when I climb into bed in case he calls back later, but I'm not optimistic. For once, I don't set my alarm. I've taken the day off work tomorrow for Lincoln's Celebration of Life service, which I promised Callie I would attend.

The following morning, there's still no response from Marco. I can't say I'm not disappointed, but I haven't given up hope. I know him. He won't let me down. He's just hurt that I lied to him and rejected his offer of help to pay for a lawyer. I'm reluctant to go down the route of retaining counsel, but it might come to that if Altman and Henry start asking too many questions or digging up dirt from my past. That's if Marco's offer still stands. I groan as I roll out of bed.

Poised in front of my closet, I drag the plastic hangers from right to left, dismissing everything in sight as too casual, too worn, too loud, or too cheap for a Bramston family Celebration of Life. Not that there's much to celebrate. Everything I've learned about Lincoln, including my suspicion that he was the man who assaulted Emma, is enough to sully his legacy as far as I'm concerned. He's not even worth the time I'm wasting trying to decide what to wear. I grab a plain navy-blue shift dress that I bought in a thrift store for a job interview and march into the bathroom to get ready.

I'm only going to this event for Callie's sake. Eleanor and Theo didn't extend an invitation to me, and I'm pretty sure if they knew I was planning on attending they would tell me not to bother.

When I pull into the funeral home parking lot, I choose a spot as far away from the building as possible. My aging Camry sticks out like a sore thumb among all the expensive late-model vehicles. I sit tight for a minute or two watching as an expensively attired couple exit their Range Rover and walk inside. I'm almost more intimidated than I was that first night I sat in the Brentdale Presbyterian Church parking lot. I have a feeling the crowd inside the funeral home won't be as welcoming as the AA group. But at least the spotlight won't be on me.

The room is packed, and I slip into an empty seat two rows from the back. Technically, I'm family, but practically I'm anything but. I'm the last person Eleanor and Theo would want to see squeezing into their roped-off seats. Several well-coiffed women hover over Callie, dabbing their eyes while furtively skirting glances around the room to see who else is in attendance. A few people throw curious glances in my direction, but no one interacts with me. One elderly gentleman dips his head when he catches my eye, then immediately looks away when the overweight woman beside him admonishes him with a not-so-subtle poke in the ribs.

I flick through the service booklet, adorned with an airbrushed photo of a beaming Lincoln in an expensive suit. I fight the urge to rip it to shreds and toss it on the empty seat

116

next to me instead. I have no intention of bringing it home as a memento.

An employee of the funeral home steps up to the microphone and reminds everyone that photography is not permitted and to please turn off their cell phones before the service begins. I take the opportunity to check one more time to see if Marco has responded, but of course he hasn't.

I turn my attention to the screen at the front of the room, parading photos from Lincoln's privileged childhood all the way through to his wedding and beyond. Soft music accompanies the masterful video montage, flanked on either side by an ostentatious display of desert roses and oriental lilies. Video cameras have been set up around the room to live stream the event. I curl my hands into fists, welcoming the pain of my nails digging into the soft fleshy part of my palms. It's a deceptively slick production to commemorate a sick individual.

Someone slips into the seat directly behind me and clears their throat, as though trying to get my attention.

I turn to look, my heart plummeting when I see who it is.

CHAPTER 37

Detective Altman stretches out a hand to shake mine. "I wasn't sure I'd see you here," he says.

"I . . . uh . . . I wanted to be here for Callie."

"Of course." Altman gestures with his chin to the front of the room. "I take it they didn't save you a seat."

I shrug. "I wouldn't expect them to. They barely know me."

He nods slowly, as though weighing the truth in my words. "I imagine it would be difficult for Eleanor and Theo to have a stranger sitting with them while they're mourning the loss of their son. They've had a harrowing time of it lately, one tragedy on top of another." He pulls his brows together. "Such a shame you and your sister didn't connect in happier times."

"I've had the same thought myself, but I feel selfish for even thinking it. This isn't about me."

"That's a noble sentiment. I can tell you care a lot about your sister."

I nod, blinking back salty tears.

"I'm sure you'd do anything for her," Altman adds, a genial smile on his face.

The hair on the back of my neck prickles. I'm suddenly unsure if his intentions are entirely empathetic. Is he here to pay his respects or is he snooping around trying to find some evidence to bring me down? Sweat beads along my hairline. I'm spared from responding when the minister appears at the podium and the music fades away.

The muted conversations in the room die down as he welcomes the mourners and acknowledges Lincoln's parents and widow.

I try to concentrate, but the accolades being lauded on Lincoln are nauseating. Either the minister has been paid handsomely for his time, or he's in the Bramston family's inner circle.

"Some of you may remember Lincoln as a colleague, others as a cousin, a friend, a boss, a board member, a son, a husband — a brilliant young man who added to the success of his father's extraordinary business ventures." The minister pauses and looks around the room, smiling at the nodding heads. "Everyone is a collection of who they were in life, and Lincoln's legacy is remarkable for the few short years he had here on earth," he continues. "I'm sure many of you will be sharing stories and memories of him at the open mic later. We also have some moving pre-recorded tributes from overseas friends and relatives that attest to Lincoln's exceptional skills and legacy."

He drones on, but each time I try to tune him out, all I can think about is Altman's eyes boring into the back of my head. Why did he sit directly behind me? There were enough other open seats at the back of the room. I can't help thinking his presence here might have less to do with the Bramstons and more to do with me. I wish I'd thought to ask Marco to come with me. I feel vulnerable without him. The very fact that he's distancing himself from me is shaking my confidence. I check my phone intermittently, but there's nothing but deafening silence on Marco's end.

Before I know it, the service has concluded. I'd like nothing more than to bail out before Altman can corner me again, but I want Callie to know that I came to support her.

"That was quite the service," Altman says, getting to his feet.

I eye him warily. "I'm not sure what that's supposed to mean. Well-orchestrated, ostentatious, surprising?"

He chuckles. "All of the above."

"There was no expense spared, that's for sure."

"I've been thinking," Altman says, cocking his head to one side and appraising me. "It must have come as quite a shock to you to discover that your sister had married into such a wealthy family."

I shrug. "It was a bigger shock to learn I had a sister to begin with."

"Some people would be envious in that situation."

I throw him a sharp look. "Is there something you want to ask me?"

His lips fashion a thin smile. "I admire your directness, but this isn't the time or the place." He reaches into his pocket and hands me his card. "Call me when you're done here. We need to talk."

CHAPTER 38

I hang around at the back of the room until the crowd begins to disperse, then make my way over to Callie. We embrace awkwardly under the watchful eye of Eleanor Bramston.

"It was a beautiful service," I mumble to no one in particular.

"Please say you'll come to the reception luncheon at the Bellingham Hotel," Callie says, taking my hands in hers.

I throw a hesitant look at Theo and Eleanor, but they've turned their backs and are engaged in conversation with another couple.

"I'm not sure I'd be welcome," I say, lowering my voice. "Your in-laws weren't exactly welcoming."

"That makes two of us," Callie replies. "I'd rather have you with me than face them alone."

I give a reluctant nod. "What's the address? I'll meet you there."

"You can ride with me. I'll drop you back here afterward." Callie leans in closer. "We can talk on the way."

I leave her to converse with the mourners waiting to express their condolences, and make my way out to the foyer.

The minute I climb into her Tesla, she turns to me. "Did you see Altman?"

121

"It was hard to miss him. He sat right behind me."

Callie throws me a worried look as she exits the parking lot. "I don't know what he was doing here. We didn't invite him."

"He doesn't need an invite. He's investigating a crime. He was on a fishing expedition."

"Did you talk to him?"

I twist my lips into a grimace. "I didn't have a choice. I tried to say as little as I could, but he kept making loaded comments."

"Like what?" Callie asks, a heightened edge of concern in her voice.

"He brought up the fact that you and I connected right around the same time Athena disappeared and Lincoln died. And he made a comment about how much I cared about you and that he was sure I would do anything for you. It was the way he emphasized the word 'anything' that spooked me. I got the feeling he wasn't simply trying to have a friendly conversation."

"Maybe you're reading too much into it," Callie says.

"I don't think so. He even insinuated I was jealous of you when I discovered you'd married into wealth. I think he was hinting that I'm now a suspect. He wants to talk to me once I'm done here."

Callie frowns. "Why you and not me?"

"He's probably giving you some space. He's hardly going to grill you the day of your husband's memorial service. I'm sure you'll be next on his call list. Just remember everything we discussed. We need to impress on him that Lincoln made a lot of enemies — any one of whom could be a potential suspect."

Callie releases a heavy breath as we pull up in front of the Bellingham Hotel. "At least he won't be at this luncheon. I need some time to pull myself together before I speak to him again."

We leave the car with the valet parking attendant and walk up the front steps. I'm painfully aware that I'm under-dressed for the occasion. The footman at the door is gracious enough not to let his gaze linger on my attire, but I can tell

122

by the way he quickly averts his eyes that it hasn't escaped his notice.

Callie and I follow the signs for the Bramston Memorial Luncheon to a large, tastefully decorated banquet hall. Yet again, no expense has been spared. Dozens of round tables adorned with white tablecloths and elaborate centerpieces are dotted around the room. Several tables are already occupied. Callie leads me to a reserved table and pats the seat next to her. "Sit here."

As I pull out the chair, I catch Eleanor Bramston glaring at me from the other side of the room.

"I'm not sure this is a good idea," I say to Callie. "Your mother-in-law doesn't look happy to see me here."

"Lincoln was my husband," Callie says, tilting her chin defiantly. "I'll have the last word on who sits at the table with me." She gets to her feet and glances around. "I need to use the restroom. I'll be right back."

My phone beeps in my purse with an incoming text and I scramble to fish it out. Finally, Marco has responded! I click on his message just as someone sits down in the chair on the other side of me.

I freeze when I see who it is.

CHAPTER 39

"Hello, Piper," Henry says, reaching for a carafe of water in the middle of the table. "Can I pour you a glass?"

"Uh, sure, thanks," I reply, scanning the room for any sign of Callie returning. Did she know Henry was going to be attending the luncheon? I didn't see him at the memorial, but it's possible I missed him in the crowd of people. When he sets the carafe back down, I reach for my glass and take a hasty gulp. "I believe this table is reserved for the Bramston family."

"Forgive me," Henry replies, turning his chair to face me. "I forgot to mention that Eleanor requested I sit with the family."

I purse my lips and shoot him a look of distain. I can hardly argue with that. Even Callie won't be able to chase him off. After all, Eleanor and Theo are footing the bill for everything.

Henry skewers me with a questioning gaze. "Where did you grow up, Piper?"

"I find it hard to believe you haven't already run a background check on me."

He chuckles. "It's always more captivating to hear people tell their story firsthand." He drapes an elbow over the back of his chair, a devious grin playing on his lips. "I find it inter-esting which parts of people's lives they choose to share and which parts they hide."

A prickle of unease runs up my spine. Is he taunting me? Does he know about the eighteen months of my life I spent locked up? Has he been tailing me to my AA meetings?

"I grew up in Southern California, near Torrance," I say. "Not far from where Callie grew up, actually."

"It's amazing the difference a ZIP code can make in the trajectory of a person's life," Henry replies, his expression an innocuous mask. "I imagine you were intimidated meeting the Bramstons for the first time."

"I'm not easily intimidated," I say coldly.

Henry looks amused. "You can't tell me you weren't at least a little envious."

"I choose not to harbor destructive emotions."

Henry nods as he crosses his legs. "Very wise. For all their money, the Bramstons are an unhappy family. What did your sister tell you about the state of her marriage to Lincoln?"

"Maybe you should ask her that."

"I want an outsider's opinion — particularly someone with good observational skills, like yourself. I'm sure you're only too eager to help in whatever way you can to get to the bottom of what happened to your sister's husband."

"Absolutely. She's all I have." I reach for my water and chug the rest of it, but it does little to lubricate my parched throat.

"How would you describe Lincoln's demeanor the night he died?"

"He wasn't too happy to see me. He thought I was after their money. He made some remarks to that effect. He pulled Callie into the family room to talk in private — next thing I know, they were arguing."

"Could you hear what they were saying?"

I struggle to hold his gaze. I'm not about to admit I was eavesdropping. "Bits and pieces. He wanted me out of the house. Callie had no choice but to ask me to leave. She was scared of him."

Henry taps his fingers on the table, his hawk-eyed gaze never leaving my face. "Was he abusive toward her?"

"He shoved her around and tried to intimidate her, but he never left any marks on her. Callie said it was mostly psychological or emotional abuse."

Henry flattens his lips. "I imagine Callie must be experiencing a certain measure of relief now that he's gone."

I tense, sensing he's baiting me. "Lincoln wasn't perfect, but he was still her husband. She's heartbroken."

"Really?" Henry says with an edge of scorn. "Did you notice either of them acting out of the ordinary that night?"

"I don't know them well enough to answer that."

Henry stretches his lips into a scathing smile. "Or maybe you're deliberately trying to mislead me."

"Why would I want to do that? Like you said, I'm only too eager to help."

Henry smirks, the look on his face telling me he doesn't believe a word I'm saying. "Your sister said she and Lincoln argued about his affair. Did it get physical at all?"

Blood drains from my face. *Not unless you count shoving your husband down a flight of stairs.* I swallow the lump in my throat. "No," I say in a breathy tone that lacks even a modicum of conviction.

I throw a desperate glance over my shoulder, relieved to see Callie making her way through the sea of tables toward us.

"I suggest we end this conversation now and show my sister a little respect," I say.

Henry straightens up in his seat. "Stall all you want. I intend to find out what happened to Lincoln Bramston, with or without your cooperation." He leans over and whispers in my ear. "Why take the fall for someone who's only using you?"

CHAPTER 40

Callie glowers at Henry as she resumes her seat. "What are you doing here?"

"Your mother-in-law invited me to sit with the family," Henry replies. "She wants me to bring her up to speed on my investigation."

He turns to me, and I feel the intensity of his gaze raking over my face. I almost feel relieved when I spot Eleanor and Theo marching over to our table.

Eleanor dismisses me with a scathing glance as she flicks her napkin open on her lap. "What a beautiful service. A real tribute to our son." She pulls out a tissue and dabs at her eyes.

Theo rests a hand on her shoulder, but she flinches beneath his touch, and he hastily withdraws it. I suspect his role is limited to underwriting the Bramston lifestyle.

Waiters appear in every corner of the room and begin a synchronized service, depositing plates of arugula, sun-dried tomatoes, toasted pine nuts, and shaved Parmesan on the tables. I throw a befuddled glance over the plethora of silverware in front of me. When Callie reaches for a small fork on the outer edge of her place setting, I follow suit.

"Henry, why don't you bring us up to date on your investigation?" Eleanor says.

I choke on the salad stuck in my throat. Henry obligingly gives me a hard pat on the back and hands me my water. "Are you okay?"

I swallow a mouthful and nod. "Yes, thank you. It went down the wrong pipe, that's all."

Eleanor raises a scolding eyebrow in my direction, before turning her attention back to Henry. "Go ahead, Faulkner."

He beams at me. "Piper and I were just discussing the fact that she grew up only an hour away from Callie."

"Worlds apart," Eleanor mutters.

"Surely it's not appropriate to be discussing the investigation into our son's death at a luncheon honoring his life," Theo says, drawing his brows together. "Someone might overhear."

"What if they do?" Eleanor snaps. "I'm not going to hide the fact that I don't accept the premise that Lincoln committed suicide. My son was murdered!"

Several heads at a neighboring table turn in our direction.

Henry stares at me, an unsettling glitter in his eyes. My heartbeat quickens. He knows something, but what? Has he found out that I've served time for attempted manslaughter? It wouldn't have been hard to get his hands on the information. Does he know what happened to Emma? Has he made a connection between her and Lincoln? I curl my hands into fists in my lap. Theo's right. This isn't the time or the place. I need to get out of here before Henry starts spilling my sorry life story to the entire table.

I reach for my phone and read Marco's message.

I want to help you.

"You'll have to excuse me," I blurt out. "I have an emergency situation." Before anyone can stop me, I jump up and start weaving my way through the tables toward the exit.

"Piper! Wait!" Callie calls out, catching up with me in the hallway. "Do you want a ride back to your car?"

I shake my head. "No. You need to be here. I'll get an Uber."

She gives a reluctant nod. "I'll let you know what Henry says about his investigation."

I grimace. "He knows I've been to prison. I saw it in his eyes."

We fall silent when a hotel manager walks into view. She gives a nod of acknowledgment in passing. When she turns the corner, we pick the conversation back up.

"What do I do if Henry tells them you've been to prison?" Callie asks, pulling nervously at her hair.

"Act like it's news to you. It doesn't change anything. Stick to our story of what happened that night."

Callie gives a miserable nod. "I'm sorry about Henry. I didn't know Eleanor had invited him, otherwise I would have warned you."

"She probably invited Altman too." I grimace. "She wants to make sure I know she has eyes on me at all times."

CHAPTER 41

The minute Callie goes back inside, I call Marco. "Can you pick me up? I'm at the Bellingham Hotel."

"Car trouble?"

"It's a long story."

"I'm on my way."

Relief floods through me. He sounds more like his old self, the curtness gone from his tone. It took him long enough, but he's obviously decided to forgive me.

I walk outside the hotel and start making my way down the lengthy driveway, away from the curious glances of the valet parking attendants. Marco pulls up next to me a short time later.

"Thanks for coming to my rescue," I say. "You must have been speeding the entire way to get here this quickly."

"I was in the area when you called. Where's your car?"

"At the Fernwood Funeral Home. I rode to the luncheon with Callie, but I left early when that PI showed up. He freaked me out."

Marco shoots me a look of concern. "What do you mean?"

"He knows something's up. He might be fishing, but he asked me why I would take the fall for someone who's only using me."

Marco lets out a long, low whistle. "So, he suspects you're helping Callie cover something up."

"That's what it sounds like. He can't possibly know exactly what happened, but he knows things aren't adding up."

"What do you need my help with?" Marco asks.

"We need to do something to deflect his attention. I need you to email him an anonymous tip suggesting a link between Athena's disappearance and Lincoln's murder."

"What kind of link?"

"I don't know. Someone could have abducted Athena and Lincoln found out who it was. He could have double-crossed a partner in a business deal or something."

Marco stares straight ahead, mulling it over.

"What do you think?" I prompt.

"I don't like the idea of involving the kid."

"You mean Athena? Why? What harm is there in that? If anything, it might put more attention on her. I can't believe they haven't found any trace of her yet. She can't simply have vanished." I shift impatiently in my seat. "Will you help me or not?"

"Yeah, sure. I can encrypt an email and use a VPN to hide the IP address. But sending an email is just a band-aid on a bigger problem. The cops are going to take a long hard look at Callie now that the autopsy has determined Lincoln was dead before his car plunged into the ravine. The spouse is always the first suspect. And you'll be next in line — you were with her the night Lincoln died."

"They can't prove anything. So long as Callie doesn't crack, we'll be fine," I say, as we pull into the funeral home parking lot. "Thanks for the ride. I'll meet you back at your place."

Marco gives a less than enthusiastic nod. If he wasn't involved enough before, he'll be right in the thick of it after this. Creating false evidence is probably some form of obstruction of justice. If he's busted, he'll never work in cyber security again.

I can't help wondering how the luncheon is going, and what Henry has told Eleanor and Theo Bramston about me.

They'll latch onto me as a suspect once they discover my criminal past.

But the truth is, I didn't harm their son — I covered for the person who did.

CHAPTER 42

"What do you want this email to Henry to say?" Marco asks, sitting down in front of one of the many computers humming away on every surface in his office.

"How about, *Lincoln Bramston's death is linked to his daughter's disappearance. You need to look at his business partners.*"

Marco turns back to the screen, his fingers flying over the keyboard. "Are you sure about this before I send it? He'll likely show it to the police."

"I don't have any better ideas. I need to do something to take the heat off me and Callie."

Marco slumps back in his chair and rubs his hands over his face.

"I'm sorry for dragging you into this," I say. "But you said you wanted to help."

He grunts. "Not this kind of help. I wanted to hire you a good lawyer. You're skating on thin ice, Piper. I can make this email untraceable, but it's like throwing a cup of water on a raging wildfire. It won't deter the cops. They'll talk to Lincoln's business partners, and look into his affairs, and when they find nothing that links his daughter's disappearance to his death, the spotlight will be back on the last two people to see him alive — his wife and her sister."

"You don't know that. They might find some dirt on Lincoln when they pull back the curtains. Wealth and corruption go hand in hand."

Marco rubs his jaw. "You watch too many movies. Theo Bramston comes from a long line of money. Whatever questionable business his grandfather might have been involved in, it was a long time ago. Theo inherited the family fortune and added to it. Lincoln was more interested in exploiting the lifestyle than contributing much of anything to it."

"How do you know all this?"

Marco gestures to the computers with a sweep of his arm. "All the information in the world is there for the taking if you know how to get your hands on it."

I furrow my brow. "Should I send Eleanor and Theo a ransom demand for their granddaughter instead?"

Marco's expression darkens. "Like I said, leave the kid out of it."

"And like *I* said, invoking her name might help find her. The police haven't made any progress. They're obviously not making her a priority. We could actually do some good if we found her in the process."

Marco runs a hand over his thinning hair. "I don't like that idea any better. A ransom demand will trigger a higher-priority investigation. We're talking FBI."

I get to my feet and pace the room. I might open us up to more scrutiny than I bargained for if the FBI get involved. Henry's a snake and Altman has plenty of experience, but neither of them have anything like the resources the Feds have at their disposal.

"All right," I say. "Stick with the anonymous tip for now."

Marco turns his attention back to the screen. A short time later, he gets to his feet and stretches. "It's done. Want something to drink?"

"Just some water, thanks."

I follow him into the kitchen and take a seat at the table.

"I really appreciate you helping me out like this," I say when he sets a glass in front of me.

He pops open a Diet Coke and takes a mouthful. "I don't know if I'm helping you or harming you. I can't stop thinking about what that PI said. You're risking everything for your sister. If she goes down, she'll take you with her."

CHAPTER 43

"How was the Celebration of Life service?" Jenna asks when I go into work the following morning.

"Over the top, like every event the Bramstons host, I imagine." I hang up my coat and reach for my apron. "The worst part was listening to the minister drone on and on about what a wonderful person Lincoln was. People don't know what he was really like."

"You didn't know him very well either. You only met the man one time, right?"

I grimace. I can't exactly tell her about the time he almost strangled me. It gives me a motive to kill him. "Once was enough. He was rude, obnoxious, and angry. My sister wanted to leave him."

"So why didn't she?"

"As you know, the Bramston family is powerful. She had to go about it the right way. She was collecting evidence."

Jenna frowns as she expertly weaves her hair into a braid. "What kind of evidence?"

"Proof of Lincoln's extramarital activities. He had several affairs — she suspected him of cheating on her with their neighbor. And she found surveillance photos he had taken of strange women. It looked like he'd been stalking them. He might even have assaulted some of them."

Jenna's brows shoot up in alarm. "Why didn't she go to the police?"

"She only found the photos a couple of days before Lincoln died. She thinks his mother destroyed them because they disappeared right after she showed them to her. Thankfully, I had managed to snap some shots of them, but they're not great quality."

"Can any of the women be identified?"

I shake my head. "It's dark and the photos are all taken from behind or from the side. Their facial features are obscured."

"How many photos were there?" Jenna asks.

"At least a dozen or more of different women."

Jenna looks shocked. "If Lincoln assaulted any of these women, it's possible he kept some mementos. Has Callie searched the rest of the house?"

"I don't think so. Their place is enormous. The cops took Lincoln's computer, but that was about it."

"Tell your sister to dig around some more." Jenna sets her lips in a grim line as she turns on the ovens to preheat. "That family is bad business."

I begin cleaning the counters and display cases, my mind racing. Jenna's right. There could be something in the house that would prove what a monster Lincoln was and confirm everything Callie said about him. I need to go by there after work and help her search the place.

I'm busy stocking the cases with baked goods when someone knocks on the front door. I glance up in irritation. We don't open for another hour. My heart lurches in my chest at the unwelcome sight of Detective Altman standing outside holding up his badge to the glass door. I forgot to call him after I left the service yesterday.

Jenna walks in from the back, wiping flour from her hands onto her apron. When she sees who it is, she shoots me an inquiring look.

I shrug. "I don't know what he wants."

"You'd better let him in."

I trudge over to the door, my feet as leaden as my heart. This must be important, or he wouldn't have come here at the crack of dawn to talk to me. At least he's not waving handcuffs at me.

I unlock the door and pull it open, keeping my expression impassive.

"Morning, Piper," Altman says, rubbing his hands together as he steps inside. "Nice and warm in here. And it sure smells good."

"Can I get you a coffee?" Jenna asks.

Altman gives her a grateful smile. "I would love one, thanks. Black, no sugar."

She looks at me and I shake my head. I'm jittery enough as it is.

"Help yourself to a freshly baked pastry," Jenna adds, before heading out back to the coffee maker.

"You never called me," Altman says.

"Sorry, I forgot all about it. Things were a little hectic yesterday."

"I understand you left the luncheon early. Some kind of emergency?" Altman asks, his eyes running over the pastries lined up in the case in front of him.

I clear my throat. "Yes, a friend needed my help."

Altman nods. "That seems to be your specialty, helping people in need."

I duck behind the display case to disguise my unease. "What can I get you?"

"I'll go with one of those blueberry muffins, thanks."

Jenna reappears with a steaming mug of coffee and hands it to Altman. "I'll leave you two to talk. I'll be out back if you need me, Piper."

"Have you made any progress on the investigation?" I ask nonchalantly.

Altman nods as he chews. "We got an interesting tip last night."

I try to keep my expression neutral. Henry must have shown them the email.

Altman washes a mouthful of muffin down with a swig of coffee. "A truck driver reported that a silver Mercedes almost rear-ended him the night Lincoln died."

I sway back on my heels, before managing to steady myself. "Really? That doesn't surprise me. Lincoln was in a foul mood that night."

"The thing is," Altman goes on, "the truck driver is adamant a woman was driving."

CHAPTER 44

My heart feels like it's ricocheting around inside my chest. I stretch my lips into a condescending smile. "Sounds about right. Callie said Lincoln was having an affair."

"True." Altman takes another bite of his muffin and chews in a deliberate fashion. The silence between us is agonizing, but I know better than to fill it with empty words. I force myself to wait patiently until he continues.

He wipes his lips with a napkin and reaches for his mug. "What do *you* think happened to your brother-in-law?" He slurps his coffee, eying me with an expectant air from beneath his brows.

"It seems pretty obvious he committed suicide. He left that email for Callie."

"You saw it?" Altman fires back. He's like a cougar waiting to pounce.

"No. Callie told me about it. I guess she'd already called you."

Altman grunts. "It didn't sound like something an abuser would write to his wife — confessing to stalking other women."

I'm tempted to tell him about Emma, and that I suspect Lincoln was the guilty party, but that gives me a motive.

"Maybe he had some remorse about his behavior," I say. "Can you imagine the outcry if the media had found out the Bramston heir was a monster who stalked women? Lincoln was a coward at heart, like every other bully. He couldn't face the consequences of his own actions."

"You're quite passionate when it comes to men who abuse women, aren't you?"

I narrow my eyes at him. "I like to think I stand up for what's right."

"You paid a price for it in the past. Eighteen months, to be exact. You did a number on that guy."

"It was an accident. He didn't deserve what happened to him, but Emma didn't deserve to have pictures of her half-naked body passed around after her death either."

"The prosecution maintained you shoved that kid down the steps."

I shrug. "His dad was a judge. I didn't stand a chance. I had a public defender."

Altman cocks his head to one side, hands wrapped around his coffee mug. "So, you wouldn't say you're prone to rash decision-making, violent outbursts, and addictive behaviors?"

I grit my teeth. He's lifted those lines straight from the psychological evaluation the state did of me — a not-so-subtle way of telling me he knows everything there is to know about me.

"I fought my battles and won. I've been clean and sober for ten years now."

"Impressive," Altman says. "I talked to your friend who attends the AA meetings with you — what's his name?" He scrunches his eyes shut as though searching through the database in his brain. "Marco something or other. Diaz — that's it. What is it he does for a living again?"

"Computers," I reply in a clipped tone.

Altman peers into his empty coffee mug and sets it aside. "Ah, yes. Cyber security. Smart kid."

"He's pretty tech-savvy." I'm getting a bad feeling about where this is going.

"You've been friends a long time, I gather."

"He was the first person I met at the AA group. If it hadn't been for him, I would have turned around and walked back out the door that first night."

"A loyal friend, then. I'm willing to bet he'd do anything for you. Just like you'd do anything for your sister." Altman's gaze bores into me. "I'm beginning to see a pattern here."

CHAPTER 45

"Is there anything else I can help you with?" I ask in a cutting tone. "I need to get to work. We're almost ready to open."

Altman folds his arms in front of him and leans back against the counter I sanitized earlier. "Forensics is processing the Mercedes right now. It will be interesting to see whose DNA we find in the car."

He raises his brows, inviting my response.

Anger wells up inside me, threatening to explode. I need to breathe and manage my emotions. "I hope you find what you're looking for." I gesture to the trays of freshly baked muffins cooling behind me. "Feel free to take one for the road if you're so inclined."

Altman pats his belly as he straightens up. "I need to stay away from those. Addictive. We all have our weaknesses." He chuckles at his parting shot as he exits the bakery.

I've barely had time to take a breath before Jenna scurries back in. "Are you okay? You're white as a sheet."

I nod, even though my insides are quaking like jelly.

"What did he want?" she asks. "I'm guessing it wasn't simply a jovial chat over a blueberry muffin and a mug of coffee."

"I think he wanted to intimidate me. He said some truck driver reported almost being rear-ended by a Mercedes driven by a female the night Lincoln died. The cops are processing the car for DNA."

Jenna's mouth drops open. "What exactly is he insinuating? That *you* were driving?"

I shrug. "Or Callie. We were both at the house the night Lincoln died. They have to rule us out as suspects."

Jenna scratches her brow. "Aren't you worried? I'd be freaking out by now. What if the cops try to frame you or something? You hear about these kinds of things happening."

"I'm not concerned about what they'll find in the car. I'm worried about how my sister's going to bear up under all this. She's just lost her husband, and now the police are looking at us as potential suspects. Not to mention the fact that Eleanor Bramston has hired a hotshot PI who's been digging up my past."

Jenna shakes her head. "I don't know why that woman doesn't focus more of her efforts on finding her granddaughter. Do you think there's a connection between Athena going missing and Lincoln turning up dead?"

I throw her a wary look. "What kind of connection?"

"I don't know. It just seems odd that two tragedies would strike a family a few weeks apart — assuming Athena didn't run away. Maybe she was abducted. Wealthy people's kids are always at risk of being kidnapped."

"The police aren't looking at that angle," I say. "They still think she's a runaway."

Jenna glances at her watch. "Time to get this place opened up." She walks over to the door to unlock it, then hesitates, one hand on her hip. "I think you might be on to something. Nobody runs away from the Bramstons. It wouldn't surprise me if something's happened to that poor girl."

I walk behind the counter and start setting out some samples. "I feel so helpless. If the Bramston family money can't find her, what chance do I stand?"

"How about creating a Facebook page?" Jenna suggests. "I'm surprised the family hasn't done it already — unless they don't want her to be found." She wags a finger at me. "I'm worried that girl never made it out of the house."

Jenna's words hang with me for the rest of the day. I need to talk to Callie and get more information about her stepdaughter. Someone needs to care enough to turn the spotlight on her and away from her worthless father. I think I can figure out how to set up a Facebook page myself, but I can always enlist Marco if I run into any problems.

"See you tomorrow," I call to Jenna when I clock out later that afternoon. I'm eager to go home and get busy doing something to help find my niece. I'll need to ask Callie for some pictures and basic information about when she was last seen and what she was wearing, but there can't be much more to it than that.

Back at my apartment, I heat up some leftover soup and drop a slice of bread in the toaster. When I open my phone, a new Facebook notification pops up.

I click on it and gasp when I read the message.

I know what you did.

CHAPTER 46

I clap a hand to my mouth, shock circulating through my system. I race through every possible name in my head trying to work out who could have sent the message. The profile looks generic — fake, most likely. I wonder if Marco could figure it out. Then a horrible thought hits me. What if he's behind it? Could he be trying to scare me into retaining a lawyer? No! He would never do something so twisted. He may be holding a grudge, but he wouldn't torture me like this. Callie's the only other person who knows what I did, but this isn't her style — she's not that subtle. I'm sure she hasn't the foggiest how to send a message from an anonymous Facebook account anyway.

Jenna encouraged me to set up a page to help locate Athena, but that doesn't mean she knows how to send anonymous messages on the platform either. Besides, she doesn't know what I did, and she'd never stab me in the back if she did.

It's possible Henry sent it. There's something creepy about the way he whispered to me at the luncheon. Could the message be referring to what I did in the past? But why would he send it? He can't be planning on blackmailing me — he knows I have no money.

And then another thought hits me. Vanessa, or Doug, or possibly both of them, could be behind it. Most likely Vanessa. If she was having an affair with Lincoln, she must be pretty cut up about his death. And if she saw someone driving Lincoln's Mercedes that night, she might have put two and two together.

I pick up my bowl of lukewarm soup and stir it absent-mindedly with a spoon. I wonder if Callie got a message too. I dip the dry toast into my soup and force myself to take a bite. It's only six o'clock. I should pay Vanessa and Doug a visit. I need to get to the bottom of this and put a stop to it before it goes any further.

I stack my dirty dishes in the overflowing sink, grab my jacket, and hurry out to the car. Marco would try and talk me out of this if he knew what I was up to, but I'm not going to tell him. Even though he's not ignoring me anymore, he still seems to be holding on to some resentment that I'm not doing things his way.

I text Callie to let her know I'm on my way, then crank up the heat in my Camry. I spend most of the drive trying to work out how to broach the subject of the anonymous message with Vanessa and Doug. They're the obvious suspects, but if I come right out and accuse them of sending it, they'll just deny it.

Callie answers the door to me in a Ralph Lauren pajama set. "I was about to take a bath when I got your text," she says, leading me to the kitchen. "What's up?"

"I had a visit from Detective Altman today. That truck driver I almost rear-ended reported seeing a female driving Lincoln's Mercedes."

Callie hugs her arms around herself, staring at me like a deer in the headlights. "But they can't prove it was you, right?"

"I was careful. They won't find my DNA in the car."

"What about cameras?" Callie asks. "Do you think they might have caught your face when we were driving through town?"

"I'm not worried about that. I kept my baseball cap pulled down low." I shrug off my jacket. "But we have another problem. I got an anonymous Facebook message this evening." I pull it up on my phone and pass it to Callie.

"*I know what you did*," she reads. "What does that mean?"

"I'm not sure. I don't know if they're referring to my past, or if someone saw us that night."

"Who?" Callie demands.

"I'm worried your neighbors, Vanessa and Doug, might have seen something. I saw the light go out in their house while I was waiting in the Mercedes for you to pull up behind me."

Callie's face pales. "Why didn't you tell me?"

"I didn't want to get ahead of myself. I figured one of them might have been using the bathroom and didn't notice the car outside. This message has made me rethink that."

Callie puckers her forehead. "But wouldn't they have said something to me — or to the cops? Could the message be from someone else?"

"Yes. It's possible Henry Faulkner could have sent it," I say. "You know what a snake he is. But I'm going to start by paying your neighbors a visit. We're not the only ones hiding secrets."

CHAPTER 47

"What are you going to say to them?" Callie asks. "You can hardly come right out and ask them if they saw you driving off with Lincoln's body."

"I'll figure something out. If they sent the message, I need to know what their endgame is. They might be planning on blackmailing us. They know you have money."

"But if it wasn't them, you're just going to raise a red flag by going over there," Callie points out.

"I'll get the information out of them without telling them anything they don't already know," I say, getting to my feet. "I'll be back shortly."

Callie throws me a disgruntled look. "This is a bad idea."

"Trust me, doing nothing is a worse idea."

* * *

Shivering in the cool night air, I jog up to Doug and Vanessa's front door and ring the bell. My pulse thuds in my temples as I wait for them to answer. If this doesn't go well, I might end up making the situation worse. But I can't risk leaving any loose ends.

The door swings open and Vanessa blinks out at me, shock spreading across her face before she quickly masks it. "Can I help you?"

"Yes. I'm Piper Madden, Callie's sister. I'd like to talk to you and Doug, if you have a minute."

"Doug's not home," Vanessa responds, attempting to close the door in my face.

"Wait!" I stick my foot out to jam it. "It's you I want to talk to anyway. It's important."

A gleam of curiosity flickers in her eyes. She sniffs and pulls the door open. "Fine. You'd better come in."

I follow her into the family room where she gestures for me to take a seat on the couch. She perches on the edge of a chair at the far end of the room and folds her arms in front of her, waiting for me to speak.

"As you can imagine," I begin, "my sister is devastated at the loss of her husband."

A small smirk appears on Vanessa's face. "I find that hard to believe."

"Why do you say that?"

"There wasn't much love lost between those two."

I fire her a withering look. "And what about between you and Lincoln?"

Vanessa's cheeks flush. "What exactly are you insinuating?"

"You and Lincoln conducted a lot of private conversations behind my sister's back."

Vanessa narrows her eyes. "Am I not allowed to talk to my neighbor in my own backyard?"

"That depends on what you were talking about."

"I don't know what specific conversations you're referring to. His daughter had gone missing. I checked in with him a couple of times to ask if there had been any progress in locating her, like a good neighbor would."

"Seems like you take quite an interest in what goes on next door. I've seen you watching me before. I waved to you once, but you ignored me."

150

"I didn't know who you were. I assumed you were the help." She frowns. "I thought you said you had something important you needed to discuss with me."

"I do." I let a slow smile spread over my lips. "You see, Vanessa, I know what you did."

Astonishment flashes across her face before she composes herself.

"What are you . . . talking about?" she stammers.

"I think you know."

"I don't. I don't know what you're talking about, or anything about you. Other than that you're Callie's sister — or at least you claim to be."

"So, if you don't know anything about me, why did you send that message?"

Vanessa blinks at me, her lips flapping open and closed. "What message?"

"Don't play games with me. If you're planning on blackmailing me, you're making a big mistake. I know all about you and Lincoln, and that information would be very interesting to the detective investigating his death."

CHAPTER 48

"Are you threatening me?" Vanessa hisses, glaring across the room.

"I'm warning you," I reply. "Stay out of my business, and I'll stay out of yours."

"You don't know what you're talking about. There was nothing going on between me and Lincoln."

"Callie found photos," I say, narrowing my eyes at her. I'll leave it to her imagination what the photos were.

A flicker of fear crosses her face. "You need to leave!" she says, getting to her feet. Her eyes dart to a wrought-iron statue on the end table next to her.

I scramble up from the couch, suddenly unsure of what she's capable of.

"How dare you come over here with your unhinged accusations!" she rants. "Lincoln said you would be trouble, and he was right. With him out of the way, you're free to bleed your sister dry. And I suppose you're trying to buy my silence by spreading ugly rumors."

"You've got it all wrong," I say. "I only want to help Callie."

"By accusing me of having an affair with her husband?" Vanessa tosses her head indignantly. "If that's your idea of

152

helping, you're seriously messed up. Now get out of my house!"

She barely waits until I'm through the front door before slamming it shut behind me. I'm shocked at how quickly she morphed into a raging pit bull. For a moment I thought she was going to reach for that statue and smash my head in with it.

I hurry back over to Callie's house, mulling over the conversation. If I had to put money on it, I'd say Vanessa genuinely didn't know about that message. But something lit her off when I mentioned photos. Maybe there really are photos of her and Lincoln somewhere in the house. It's exactly the kind of evidence I need to take the heat off Callie and me.

"How did it go?" Callie asks, pulling nervously at her collar.

"Doug wasn't there. I talked to Vanessa. Judging by her reaction, I don't think she was the one who sent the message, but she was rattled when I told her I knew about her and Lincoln. I mentioned that we'd found photos — I insinuated they were of the two of them. She went ballistic and threw me out of the house. She's definitely afraid something might come to light — evidence of their affair, I'm guessing. We need to search for it."

Callie looks dubious. "If Lincoln had photos, they're most likely on his computer. And the police have that."

"He might have printed them out like he did with the surveillance photos — sicko that he was."

Callie looks away, an injured expression on her face.

"I know it's hard to hear," I say. "But at the end of the day he was a sleazeball."

"I don't miss him," she says quietly. "But the betrayal stings."

"Then put your energy into proving he was having an affair. If we find photos of Vanessa, it will be the leverage we need to make sure she keeps her mouth shut."

Callie braces herself. "Where do you want to begin?"

"Lincoln's office is the most obvious place to stash something he doesn't want found," I say.

We spend the next hour combing through every nook and cranny in his opulent office. We can't find the keys to his desk or file drawers anywhere, so we resort to breaking the locks. Flipping through all the paperwork turns out to be a tedious, painstaking process. It mostly consists of financial statements and copies of business contracts. The numbers on the paperwork are mind-boggling. I can't help wondering how much of this jackpot Callie has access to.

"There's nothing here," she says, throwing her hands up in defeat after slamming the bottom drawer of the filing cabinet shut.

"Let's move on to his closet," I say.

Callie searches through the plastic tubs on the shelves while I check the pockets of the jackets and pants hanging up. I can't resist running my fingers over the sleek suits, admiring the quality and cut. I can't imagine what it's like to walk around dressed in thousands of dollars' worth of expensive clothing. No wonder wealthy people strut through life like they own it.

"There's nothing in here either," Callie says wearily. "Ticket stubs, old watches, sports memorabilia. We're wasting our time."

"We're not done yet. The attic's next."

"I never go up there. The only things we keep in the attic are Christmas decorations."

"Which is exactly why we should search it."

After some wrangling, Callie finally succeeds in activating the electric stairs that extend down from the access point to the attic. "You go up," she says, waving me forward. "I'm allergic to dust."

I'm pretty sure she's allergic to work, but I don't contradict her. I'd rather check the attic myself anyway. I don't trust her to do a thorough job.

The light comes on automatically when I reach the top of the stairs. Callie was right, there's nothing up here but a stack of plastic tubs of Christmas decorations in one corner. I walk over to them and rummage halfheartedly through a couple. I'm beginning to think Lincoln must have kept any illicit photos of his neighbor in an encrypted file on his computer. Marco might have been able to retrieve them if the police hadn't taken the computer.

Disappointed, I duck down and make my way back over to the access point. I'm about to climb back down the ladder when something catches my eye.

"Almost done," I call to Callie, before picking my way over to the far end of the attic.

Peeking out from the insulation between the rafters is a yellow manila envelope.

CHAPTER 49

I reach for the envelope and shake out the contents. A single card flutters down to my feet. I snatch it up, my eyes widening when I read the text on the front.

Happy birthday, baby, from the best decision you ever made!

I flip open the card and suck in a sharp breath.

I love you more. I can't wait until we can be together. Your X factor.

There's nothing to indicate who the card is from, but, obviously, Lincoln's X factor is someone he was keeping hidden from Callie. I'd like to see the look on Vanessa's face when I show her this. She's not good at hiding her emotions, so it shouldn't be too hard to figure out if the card's from her.

"Are you almost done up there?" Callie yells.

"Coming!" I call back. I pull up some of the surrounding insulation to make sure there's nothing else stashed beneath it, then climb back down and hand the card to Callie. "I found this hidden under the insulation."

She reads it, taking a few heaving breaths as though she's about to have a panic attack.

"I knew he was cheating again," she says, stomping off in the direction of the kitchen.

When I join her, she's pouring herself a glass of wine. "Want one?"

I shake my head. "No, thanks."

She takes a couple of gulps and frowns, chewing on her bottom lip. "I'm such a fool. I feel like marching over there and confronting Vanessa myself."

I raise my brows. "That wouldn't end well. You're too keyed up right now. What you need to do is lock this card in your safe. Consider it fire insurance."

"So what now?" Callie asks.

I slide onto a barstool and rest my elbows on the island. "Now we wait. In the meantime, I've been thinking it would be a good idea to set up a Facebook page to help find Athena."

Callie frowns. "I'm pretty sure Eleanor's PI would have advised her to do that by now if it were important."

"It can't hurt."

Callie sips her wine. "Eleanor posted about it on her feed. She wanted me to, but I thought it was too macabre." She shudders. "And Lincoln wasn't on Facebook. 'Wastebook' he always called it."

"It would look good on your part to do something to try and find your stepdaughter. It will seem odd if you don't make an effort, especially now that Lincoln's gone."

Callie shrugs. "I don't know the first thing about setting up a Facebook page. Lincoln's assistant set up mine for me."

"It's not hard. I can do it. I just need a few recent photos of Athena and some basic information."

Callie starts scrolling through her phone. "I'll airdrop you some pictures. What kind of information do you need?"

"A physical description, what she was wearing when you last saw her — that kind of thing."

I get to work on my phone setting up a new Facebook page and title it: *Help us find Athena Bramston*. I upload the pictures Callie sends me, and fill in her stepdaughter's age, height, weight, eye color, and hair color.

"So, the last time you saw her was when she went to bed that night, correct?" I ask.

"Yes. We were watching a movie until eleven thirty or so."

"What was she wearing?"

"Jeans, black Birkenstock boots, and a pink, long-sleeved Rolling Stones shirt. It's all in the police report. But I don't know for sure if that's what she was wearing when she left the house."

"We'll run with that," I say, typing the information in. "Do you have a police report number I can include?"

Callie frowns at her phone. "Give me a minute. I can pull it up." She rattles it off and I add it, along with the phone number for the police department, and my name and relationship to Athena.

"Done!" I say, leaning back in my chair. "Now, I just need you to share the page with all your friends and ask them to share it with theirs. Hopefully, some tips will start to trickle in before too long." I glance at the time on my phone. "I should get going. I have work in the morning."

Five minutes later, I'm pulling out of Callie's driveway, but instead of heading home, I turn left. There's someone else I need to pay a visit to tonight.

CHAPTER 50

It's almost nine thirty by the time I get to Marco's place. I should really be home getting ready for bed. I have a five o'clock start in the morning. But Marco's a night owl. Knowing him, he'll either be playing video games or working into the early hours for clients. If Vanessa didn't send me that Facebook message, I'm going to need his help to find out who it was.

I lift my hand to ring the doorbell, but he pulls the door open before I get a chance. "Saw you on the camera," he says, ushering me inside. "Heard anything more from Detective Altman?"

"No. I'm going with the theory that no news is good news."

"Don't get too comfortable. You know he's working the case behind the scenes. He'll be back with more questions before you know it. Do you want something to drink?"

"I'll take a Diet Coke if you have one."

"I always save the last one for you."

I flash him a grateful smile as he tosses me a can. If I didn't know better, I'd say he was flirting with me.

"What's up?" he asks. "It's not like you to drop by this late."

"I need your help with something."

He pulls the tab on a can of Sprite. "Computer related, I'm guessing."

"Sort of. I got a disturbing Facebook message from an anonymous account." I watch him closely for any sign of guilt or evasion, but he looks genuinely surprised at the news. Unlike me, he's never been very good at lying.

"What did it say?" he asks.

"*I know what you did.*"

Marco sets down his soda and rubs a hand over his jaw. I can see the gears in his brain working. He's likely asking himself the same question I asked. Does it refer to what I did in the past — which is public record — or does someone know what happened with Lincoln?

"Did Callie get a similar message?"

I shake my head. "Just me. How hard is it to set up an anonymous account?"

Marco reaches for his Sprite. "Not hard."

"Could you trace it — find out who it is?"

"It would be a challenge. And there are ethical and legal considerations. Technically I'd be breaching privacy laws. The cops could get a subpoena and force Facebook to divulge the information."

He sips his soda. "Why are you looking at me like that? You didn't think it was me, did you?"

I shrug. "I thought you might have been trying to scare me into seeking legal counsel. I feel like you're still distancing yourself from me."

He drops his gaze. "If I am, it's to protect myself. I know it makes you uncomfortable to hear, but I care about you. I don't want to lose you."

"You're not going to lose me. Nothing's changed, Marco."

"Everything's changed. Someone knows what you've done."

CHAPTER 51

There's a strange buzzing inside my stomach as I go about my work the following morning. I'm not sure what to make of Marco's admission that he doesn't want to lose me. Does our friendship mean something more to him? It would explain why he's been acting strangely lately — distancing himself one minute and hovering over me the next. Urging me not to jeopardize my future to protect my sister but risking his for me. Last night has left me feeling disoriented. Our friendship is an anchor in my life, and I can't afford to lose it.

It doesn't sound as if Marco's going to be able to help me track down the anonymous Facebook user. The one good thing to come out of my visit is that I'm one hundred percent certain he wasn't behind the cryptic message.

I'm eating lunch out back at the Wicked Scone when Altman calls. So much for *no news is good news*. I'm tempted to ignore him, but I'd only be delaying the inevitable.

I swallow a bite of my ham and cheese sandwich and fake a bright tone. "Detective, what can I do for you?"

"Morning, Piper. I'd like you to come down to the station today. We just need to clear a few things up."

I grip the phone a little tighter, trying to keep the wobble out of my voice. "Can it wait until after work? I'm off at four."

"Sure. See you then."

I hang up and flop back in my chair, letting out an exaggerated sigh of relief.

"Everything all right?" Jenna asks, waltzing into the room.

"That was Detective Altman," I say, getting to my feet. "He wants me to go down to the station. Not sure what it's about."

Jenna purses her lips. "Do you need to take off early?"

"No. I figure it can't be too important, or he would have wanted me to come in right away."

Jenna leans against the table and checks her phone. "I saw you got the Facebook page up and running for Athena. I've been sharing it with my circle of friends. Hopefully, someone will come forward with information before something happens to that poor girl."

I give her a weak smile. In my heart of hearts, I'm afraid something has already happened to her, but I'm not going to crush the hope that she'll be found alive.

"Got any plans after work?" Jenna asks. "Other than your visit with Altman?"

"I have group tonight," I say, rumpling my brow at the thought.

Jenna raises an eyebrow. "You said that with a sense of dread."

"Not really. It's just . . ." I trail off, unsure if it's wise to say any more until I've sorted out my feelings about Marco.

The expression on Jenna's face softens. "Is this about your *friend*?" she asks, demoing emphatic air quotes.

My cheeks heat up. "I didn't realize I was such an open book."

"You two didn't have a falling out or something, did you?"

"No, but things are a little awkward at the moment. He told me last night he was scared of losing me. It sounded like a loaded statement."

"That can't have come as a surprise," Jenna says, a hint of amusement in her voice. "He's like a lovesick puppy every time he's within a mile of you. What's the hesitation?"

162

I shrug. "I value his friendship too much to risk it with a romance that might not last."

Jenna lets out a humph. "Well, it won't if you start out on such a negative note. You can't win in life if you never roll the dice. Aren't you attracted to him? He's a good-looking guy. Although, he is going bald and he's a bit of an egghead, so . . ."

I burst out laughing, and Jenna chuckles too. "Don't tell him I said that. No amount of chocolate muffins will make up for it."

"I should get back to work," I say, getting to my feet.

Jenna waves a finger playfully at me. "Think about what I said."

* * *

I pull into the police station later that afternoon, my mind still focused on Marco. Our relationship can't go anywhere until I resolve the mess I'm in. Marco's stuck his neck out enough for me already. He's risked his career; I can't have him risking his freedom too.

Inside the station, I check in with the front desk officer and take a seat. Altman appears a few minutes later and leads me to an interview room. I'm slightly uneasy at the stark surroundings. It feels too formal a setting for a few questions to clear up some loose ends.

"Can I get you something to drink — water, coffee?" Altman asks.

"No, thanks. I have a meeting tonight, so I'm a bit pressed for time. If we could just get this over and done with as quickly as possible, that would be great."

"Gotcha. I'll get right down to it. Forensics has finished processing Lincoln's Mercedes." He drums his fingers on the table in front of him. "It seems the truck driver was right about the female driver. We found several strands of long hair in the vehicle."

CHAPTER 52

"That's not surprising," I say, bolstering my tone. "Like I told you already, Lincoln was a serial cheater. I can only imagine how many women have been in his car."

Altman interlocks his fingers in front of him, nodding in agreement. "A wide-open pool. Which is why we'd like to begin by eliminating you and your sister."

I swallow the growing lump in my throat. The DNA can't be mine, not after all the precautions I took, but the thought of Callie falling under suspicion makes my skin crawl. "Isn't it logical to think my sister's DNA would be in the vehicle? She was married to the man, after all. I'm sure she drove the Mercedes from time to time."

"You're correct. We can eliminate your sister."

"That makes sense," I say, feeling slightly better about the situation. "I'm happy to provide a sample."

"Great. Let's get this over and done with so you can be on your way," Altman says. "I'll just grab a couple of things to collect the sample. Be right back."

The minute he exits the room, I shoot Marco a text.

Altman's collecting a hair sample from me.

His answer pops up almost immediately.

Decline. Request a lawyer.

I grimace. I should have known he would tell me to lawyer up. I tap out a quick reply.

See you at group.

Before he can respond, Altman returns with a sealed package in hand. He dons a pair of gloves, then pulls out some tweezers. "I promise this won't hurt as much as it looks. I just need to get the roots."

"Go for it," I say, plastering on a smile.

I wince when he yanks the hairs out, but it's over in seconds. He places the sample in a container, then seals and labels it. "All done, you're free to go."

"How long will it take to get the results?"

"Not long." His gaze drills into me, and I avert my eyes as I reach for my purse. It doesn't matter how long it takes to process the sample, he's not obligated to share the results with me anyway.

Back in my car, I glance at my phone. There's nothing more from Marco, but I have a new Facebook Messenger notification. My heartbeat ratchets up a notch as I tap on it.

Silence is costly. Bring an envelope with $5,000 cash at midnight.

Acid froths in my stomach. The pinned location attached to the message is in the middle of nowhere. I had a bad feeling that the first anonymous message might lead to this. Granted, it's not an earth-shattering amount, but it might as well be. It's more than I have at my disposal. But it's also a lot less money than Callie's neighbors would be likely to ask for. Five thousand dollars wouldn't make a difference in Doug and Vanessa's world. Have I been homing in on the wrong people?

I rub my hands over my face, conflicted about what to do and who to trust. I can't tell Marco about this. I'll have to skip group tonight. He'll insist I go to the police. There's only one thing I can do.

Go to the drop-off point and find out who's behind this.

CHAPTER 53

For the second time in years I skip group. I agonized over the decision, but I just can't face Marco right now. He'll know the minute he sees me that something's wrong. He'll offer to front me the money, but I can't accept it. I don't want to be indebted to him any more than I already am. I'm going to hit Callie up for it instead. After all, I'm in this mess because of her. And I'll insist she comes with me tonight to drop it off. She won't make as good a bodyguard as Marco, but there's safety in numbers. At least that's what I'm telling myself. The truth is, she could end up being more of a liability.

I don't bother texting Marco to tell him I'm not going to group. He'll bombard me with messages wanting to know why, and what's wrong, and he might end up skipping himself and driving around to my place. When he discovers I'm not there, he'll guess I'm with my "shiny new sister," as he calls her. The last thing I need is for him to show up at Callie's place and make a scene.

I call her number to make sure she's home. "I need to talk to you. I'm on my way."

She sighs. "Seriously? I was about to head out to Pilates. Can't it wait?"

"Not unless you can see yourself doing wall Pilates in a six-by-eight-foot cell for the next decade of your life," I say through gritted teeth.

There's a long silence on the other end before she responds. "Fine. I'll cancel."

I crank up the Camry and drive across town to Callie's swanky neighborhood. I should have gone home first and grabbed a sweatshirt or a coat for my stakeout, but I'm sure Callie has a closetful to choose from. She can whine all she wants about getting her designer duds dirty — it's the least of my concerns right now.

Thirty minutes later, I pull into her driveway. She answers the door dressed in white jeans and a cashmere sweater, and clutching a glass of wine in a way that suggests it isn't her first. I grimace. An inebriated partner is not what I was banking on. Knowing Callie, she'll fall asleep on the way and be of no help. If I end up bringing her, I'm going to have to drive and act as lookout. I'm beginning to wish I'd asked Marco to come with me instead.

"Did Altman contact you today?" I ask, following her into the family room.

Callie blinks at me blankly, then her face clears. "Oh, yes, he did. He wanted a hair sample."

"That doesn't concern you at all?"

She flaps a hand and giggles. "It's nothing to worry about. It's just routine."

"Nothing's ever routine in a murder investigation," I say through gritted teeth. "You need to take this more seriously. Has Henry Faulkner been sniffing around lately?"

"You haven't heard?"

"Heard what?"

"Eleanor fired him."

My jaw drops. "Why?"

"He billed her for all sorts of extra charges, and he tried to up his hourly rate."

"Wasn't he already getting an exorbitant rate?"

Callie shrugs. "Apparently, it wasn't enough."

I frown, digesting this new information. Could Henry be the one trying to blackmail me?

"What did you want to talk to me about?" Callie asks, barely glancing up from her phone.

"I got another message from that anonymous Facebook account. They're demanding money."

Her head jerks up in my direction. "How much?"

"Five thousand dollars. I'm willing to bet that won't be the end of it. After what you just told me about Henry, I'm now wondering if he could be behind it."

I hand her my phone so she can read the message for herself.

"Whoever's doing this must know you have money," I say. "They're counting on me asking you for the cash. We need to go to the drop-off location tonight and find out who's behind it. Can you get the money together in time?"

She shakes her head. "All the accounts were in the family trust. Eleanor froze them. She's monitoring every penny I spend."

I scrub my hands over my face. "We can't go without the cash."

"I have something better," Callie says. She reaches beneath a cushion on the couch and pulls out a gun.

169

CHAPTER 54

Callie waves the gun in my direction, still clutching her wine glass in her other hand.

"Are you crazy?" I yell, ducking out of range. "Don't point that thing at me."

She laughs, setting the gun down clumsily on the glass coffee table in front of her. "It's not loaded, you doofus."

"Like you would know. You've been drinking. Where did you get it from?"

"It was Lincoln's — it's mine now. He kept it in the drawer in his bedside table." She sets down her glass, slopping wine over the side, but doesn't appear to notice. "Lincoln was paranoid after Athena disappeared — he was afraid someone might breach the alarm and break in. He started sleeping with the gun next to him."

"We're not bringing it with us tonight," I say. "We're not going to be shooting anyone."

Callie scowls. "What if the blackmailer has a gun? They're not going to be too happy with us when they discover we don't have their money."

"They won't know until after they open the envelope. We'll drop it off early, then hide out and watch who shows up to collect it. You do have envelopes, right?"

Callie gets to her feet, a disgruntled look on her face. "I'll look in Lincoln's office."

When she exits the room, I check my phone. Nothing from Marco, but I do have a new Facebook notification. Not a message this time — it's a comment on the Facebook page I set up.

> *I saw a young woman matching Athena's description the night she disappeared. My husband and I were heading out of state on a camping trip and we stopped to gas up at the Chevron station in Elcadia Hills. I got out to use the restroom and walked right by a black Suburban. The woman was in the passenger seat, and she appeared to be asleep. I noticed her Rolling Stones shirt because that was my favorite band when I was younger. We didn't realize until we got back that she'd been reported missing.*

My heart picks up pace. This sounds like a real lead. Could Athena be in Elcadia Hills — only an hour from home. Or was she just passing through?

I quickly type out a reply:

> *Thank you so much for reaching out. Did you happen to get the license plate, or did you notice anything else about the vehicle — damage, bumper stickers or the like?*

A minute or two later, a response pops up:

> *I wish I could say I did. I didn't think to pay much attention to the vehicle.*

Callie trudges back into the room and tosses me an envelope before sinking down on the couch. "I'm too tired to go anywhere tonight. Why don't we just ignore the blackmailer — call their bluff and see what happens?"

"We can't ignore them. What if they go to the police and say they saw us leaving the property that night in two vehicles and returning in one? Do you really want to take that chance?"

Callie rolls her eyes. "Fine, I'll go with you, but we're bringing the gun and that's final. You can keep it in your purse, as you're the sober one."

I give a reluctant nod, checking to make sure the safety's on when she passes it to me. "We can't afford any more *accidents*," I say, giving her a pointed look.

Callie's eyebrows rise a touch, but she says nothing. She got the message. I'm in deep enough.

I glance at the time on my phone. "We don't have to leave for another hour or so. Got anything to eat?"

"A deli sandwich I picked up earlier."

"Works for me," I say, following her into the kitchen.

She hands me half a sandwich on a plate, and I tuck in, instantly feeling reenergized. "You should eat too," I say. "We could have a long night ahead of us."

"I'm not hungry," she replies, pushing her plate aside.

I devour the rest of my sandwich, then reach for a napkin. "Did you see we got our first real lead on the Facebook page I set up to find Athena?"

Callie's eyes widen. "No. What kind of lead?"

I pull up the page on my phone and check the message again. "A woman reported seeing someone who looked like Athena in the passenger seat of a black Suburban the night she disappeared. Do any of her friends drive a black Suburban?"

"Not that I know of. Did the woman give a description of the driver?"

"No. She just noticed the girl — she said she appeared to be sleeping, but it's possible she could have been drugged. She might have been lured online by some pervert pretending to be in love with her. You know how susceptible these young girls are."

Callie turns pale. "Lincoln was afraid something like that had happened."

"It's a bummer the woman didn't get the license plate," I say. "But we can pass the tip on to the police. It might be enough to convince them she's in danger."

Callie furrows her brow. "I doubt it. It doesn't sound like she was in the car against her will."

"Maybe Altman can get a hold of the gas station CCTV and find out who the driver was."

"Maybe," Callie says, sounding disinterested. She gets to her feet. "I need to change. I'm not wearing my cashmere sweater on a stakeout."

"Bring a flashlight, and a coat for me," I call after her.

She totters down the hallway to her bedroom, and I turn my attention back to my phone. I have another notification on Athena's page. I tap on it with a beat of excitement and read the message.

I have some information about Athena, but I can't post it on Facebook. Message me back with a number to reach you at.

173

CHAPTER 55

I reread the message, my initial excitement dimming. It could be a scam. I have no intention of giving my number out willy-nilly to some unidentified person hiding behind an anonymous post on Facebook. They might try to hack my account or steal my identity — best not to engage. I deliberate for only a moment or two, then delete the message and close the app just as Callie reappears. I groan inwardly when I see what she's wearing. She's decked out in stylish black leggings, white-and-gold sneakers that look like they've never seen the light of day before, a soft-knit gray hoodie, and a fur-lined Parka. I'm guessing she doesn't own any old clothes.

"Ready?" I ask.

"I guess so." She tosses me a down jacket.

"Thanks. Did you find a flashlight?"

"It's in my purse."

"Are you sure you want to go dressed like that?" I ask, my gaze traveling over her outfit. "We're not going to the gym. We might have to army crawl through a ditch, for all I know."

Callie pulls a face. "Very funny. I'll wait in the car if you go all hardcore military on me."

I grunt. "You're the one who wanted to bring the gun. All I'm saying is that we need to be prepared for anything. We're not going on a field trip."

"I'm well aware of that," Callie says, her Chanel purse dangling from her arm. "Do you want me to drive?"

I arch a contemptuous eyebrow at her. "Definitely not. Neither of us is going to drive. It would be too hard to hide the car once we get there. We'll take an Uber."

Callie's mouth falls open. "You're joking, right? What if we can't get an Uber back home afterward? We'll be stuck in the middle of nowhere in the pitch black of night."

I pull my lips into a tight line. "I have a Plan B if we need it."

"What's your plan B?" Callie asks, dubiously.

"A friend."

She shakes her head in disbelief. "You're going to call a friend in the middle of the night?"

I shrug, turning my attention to booking a ride. "He's a night owl."

* * *

Seated in the back of our Uber, Callie starts scrolling through her phone. "No more leads on the Facebook page." She lets out a huff. "It's so disappointing. People don't care about anything but themselves these days."

I open my mouth to tell her about the message I deleted, but change my mind. She might get mad at me for not pursuing it. She's too inebriated to be logical. And right now, I need her to stay calm.

By the time we reach the turnoff leading to the pinned location, Callie is snoring. I elbow her in the ribs and she jerks upright. "What? Are we here?" Her head swivels as she blinks herself awake. "Are you sure this is the right place?"

"Positive," I say, opening my door. I don't bother telling her that I had the Uber driver stop at the turnoff.

He peers at us over his shoulder. "Are you two going to be okay out here by yourselves?"

"We're meeting friends," I reply glibly. "They're picking us up at the junction."

The driver shrugs. "Suit yourselves."

Callie climbs out, dragging her white-and-gold heels. She shivers in the cold night air as our driver accelerates and drives off. "Where to?" she asks, turning on her flashlight.

"Up this road," I say, pointing into the shadows. "It's not far — quarter mile at most."

"Ugh! I'm too tired to walk. Why didn't you have him take us all the way?"

"I didn't want to get him involved. The less he knows, the better."

We're only a few steps in before Callie starts whining about blisters.

"Keep your voice down," I say, glancing around nervously.

"I can't believe I let you talk me into this," she fumes.

"Don't forget who got us into this mess to begin with," I shoot back.

She blows out a frustrated breath and we continue in silence for several more minutes.

"I think this is the place," I say, stopping in front of a cattle gate and checking my phone again. "Got that envelope?"

Callie rummages around in her purse and pulls it out.

"Put a rock on it so it doesn't blow away," I say.

Callie places it in front of the gate and secures it with a stone. "Now what?" she asks, rubbing her arms briskly. If nothing else, the biting night air appears to have sobered her up some.

"Now we settle in," I reply, gesturing to a grove of trees on the other side of the road. "Let's see who shows up to collect the money."

CHAPTER 56

We spend the next hour trying to stay warm while I do my best to keep Callie quiet. Midnight comes and goes without any sign of anyone.

"Maybe it was just a sick joke," she says, shivering. "Let's get out of here."

"Not yet. The blackmailer might want to make sure we've come and gone before they show up to collect their money."

Callie moans and pulls her coat tighter around her. "This is ridiculous."

By 1:30 a.m. she's had enough. "C-call your friend to come pick us up right now. If you don't, I'm wa-walking out of here and flagging d-down the nearest car." I'm not sure if she's about to burst into tears or if she's having difficulty forming the words because her lips are half frozen. Either way, our stakeout is a bust.

I hit Marco's number on speed dial and press the phone to my ear. He answers immediately so I know he's parked in front of his computer screens, headphones on. "What's up?"

"Are you working?" I ask.

"Playing. Why aren't you sleeping?"

"Callie and I need a ride home. I can send you a pin of our location."

"Car trouble again?" Marco asks, a hint of amusement in his voice.

"Something like that." I'm not going to get into it with him on the phone. He'll chew me out once I tell him what we were up to, but I'm too cold to stand here arguing about it. I'd rather have it out with him in the comfort of his car with the heater cranked up.

"How long 'til he gets here?" Callie demands.

I try to tamp down my frustration at her never-ending sense of entitlement. "He's forty minutes out."

She groans. "I'll be dead by then. I can't feel my toes anymore."

"Let's start walking in that direction," I suggest. "That way we won't have to amputate your feet later."

* * *

By the time Marco's car pulls up alongside us, Callie is in full hobble mode. The minute she falls onto the back seat, she pulls off her sneakers. "I have blisters the size of planets on my heels."

I give a dismissive grunt. "That's what you get for wearing brand-new shoes."

"Where's your car?" Marco asks me.

"Like I said, it's a long story."

He shoots me a quizzical look. "Do you want to tell me what you're doing out here in the middle of nowhere in the dead of night?"

"Can we talk about it later, in private?"

"If you insist," he replies stiffly.

My stomach knots. This latest escapade isn't going to do anything to help repair our relationship.

"So, how do you two know each other?" Callie asks, rubbing her feet.

"We've been friends a long time," I say.

Marco glances in the rear-view mirror at Callie. "What she meant to say is that we met at an AA meeting."

"How cute," Callie simpers. "Two lovebirds with broken wings find each other."

I shoot her an annoyed look. "Like I said, we're friends."

"Whatever," she replies, leaning back against the seat and closing her eyes.

Marco doesn't appear to be in the mood for conversation either. He keeps his eyes forward and his hands on the wheel. He's probably ticked off that he had to come out in the middle of the night to pick me up, but even more frustrated that I won't tell him what I was doing.

I pull out my phone and check the Facebook page again. To my surprise, there's another message.

This is Michaela Rice, Athena's friend. I'm not sure if you got my first message. Is there a number I can reach you at?

I suck in a silent breath. Could this be a legitimate lead after all? Or is someone impersonating Athena's friend online? Could it be the same person who lured me out here? After spending several hours defying hypothermia, I'm leery of messaging back without checking this person out first, especially after receiving that threat from a generic account. I tap on Michaela's profile. She's a friend of Athena's, but her Facebook page is set to private. I have no way of knowing if the message is from her or if someone has hacked her account.

I grimace, wrestling with my decision. As Jenna says, you can't win in life if you never roll the dice. I throw a quick glance across at Marco, then type my phone number into a reply and hit send.

CHAPTER 57

Marco drops us off at Callie's house and takes off immediately, after turning down her offer of a bed for the night. I give her back her gun and make sure she locks it in the safe before I leave. I barely have the energy to drive home. I'd like nothing more than to crash in her guest suite, but I have to go to work in a few short hours.

When I jolt awake later that morning, it's no surprise that I've slept past my alarm. I scramble for my phone to call Jenna, apologizing profusely for my tardiness.

"Don't worry about it," she says. "You've never been late before. Everyone gets one free pass."

"I can be there in thirty minutes," I say, fishing around in a drawer for some clean underwear.

"You sound exhausted. Why don't you take the day off? You haven't used any of your vacation days yet."

I hate to leave Jenna solo, but I could really use the time to figure out what to do about the blackmailer. I feel like I'm slowly drowning in a whirlpool of my own making.

"You know," I say, slamming the drawer shut. "I think I'll take you up on that."

There's a long pause before Jenna asks, "Is everything all right?"

"Yes. I . . . uh . . . it's just that I got a couple of leads on the Facebook page I set up to help find Athena. I need to connect with Detective Altman and persuade him to follow up on them."

"Oh, Piper, that's wonderful news. Please keep me posted if you hear anything about your niece."

She hangs up, and I see I've three missed calls — all from the same number. Could this be Michaela? A flutter of excitement stirs in the pit of my stomach. I stagger to the kitchen to pop a coffee pod into my Keurig. Mug in hand, I retreat to my lumpy couch and sink down on it. Do I wait for another call, or take the initiative and call her back? I should take a shower first. If Michaela wants to meet up, I need to be ready.

As I'm shampooing my hair, my thoughts turn to Marco. He's circumspect by nature, but not to the extreme he's been of late. I'm entirely to blame for the sorry state of our relationship. I lied to him, pushed him away, hid things from him, took risks he didn't approve of, rejected his offers of help, then demanded his help at the most inopportune times — always putting Callie ahead of him. He's probably feeling as though I've replaced him with my sister. I need to do better.

After toweling off and dressing, I turn my attention to the next-to-impossible task of assembling a nutritious breakfast from the dregs of my refrigerator. I end up slicing my last cheese stick and attempting to melt it under the broiler on top of the heel of a loaf. I manage to brown it up but it stubbornly refuses to melt. I make a mental note to go grocery shopping before the day is out.

When I'm done with my lackluster meal, I dial the unknown number and wait with bated breath.

Your call has been forwarded to voicemail. The person you are trying to reach is not available.

I groan and hang up. I don't want to leave a message when I can't be sure it's really Michaela I'm calling. I try Callie next, but she doesn't answer either. She's probably sleeping off the effects of her wine binge and blistered heels. I might as well drive over there so we can discuss our next steps. I'll pick up some groceries on the way back.

It's almost ten in the morning by the time I reach her house. There's a dark green Range Rover and a white Mercedes parked in the driveway.

I hurry up the front steps and ring the doorbell. When the door swings open, I find myself staring at the last person I want to see.

CHAPTER 58

"Can I help you?" Eleanor Bramston asks in the most condescending tone imaginable.

"I'm here to see my sister," I say with a strained smile.

She turns and marches down the hallway, heels clicking like a metronome. I take that as a summons to follow and step inside, closing the door behind me. I make my way to the kitchen and glance around, but there's no sign of Callie.

"Your sister's unavailable," Eleanor says, gesturing for me to take a seat at the table.

"Is she still sleeping?" I ask.

"Theo has taken her to our house. I'm in the process of packing her bags. She's not doing well emotionally or mentally." Eleanor's eyes bore into me like a drill. "Catering to your demands is adding to her stress."

I gasp in protest. The very idea of Callie catering to me is laughable. I'm the one who's been bending over backwards to save her skin. "What's that supposed to mean?"

Eleanor attempts to draw her tattooed brows together in her frozen forehead. "You've been guilting Callie into doing things that have further traumatized her at a time when she's already grieving the death of her beloved husband. Not to

183

mention the fact that you added to our family's pain by setting up a public Facebook page to find Athena without our permission! I've been spearheading the investigation into my granddaughter's disappearance, and I've hired the best in the business to get it done. I don't need some *stranger* interfering by plastering our drama all over the internet."

"You fired Henry, and you're conveniently overlooking the fact that I'm Athena's aunt and Callie's sister."

"Technically, but not practically. You don't know them, and we don't know you. You've taken advantage of our distress to exercise undue influence over Callie at the most vulnerable time of her life. That ends today. I don't want you contacting our family again."

"You can't stop me from seeing my sister."

"She doesn't want to see you anymore."

"I don't believe you."

Eleanor folds her hands primly in her lap. "I think it's best if you leave now."

"You can't throw me out of my sister's house. If Callie doesn't want me here, she can tell me herself." I whip out my phone and dial her number.

It rings and rings and goes to voicemail.

"As I said," a tight-lipped Eleanor continues, "she no longer wants anything to do with you. You're dangerous, and she doesn't feel safe around you."

An image of Callie with a glass of wine in one hand while waving a gun at me with the other flashes to mind. This is the same woman who accidentally shoved her husband down a flight of stairs. If anything, she's the loose cannon, and I'm the one who shouldn't feel safe. I can't believe Callie doesn't want anything more to do with me. Eleanor Bramston's a manipulative liar. She must have threatened Callie with something — most likely cutting off her money. It's like a drug to her. She can't function without it.

"If you don't leave quietly, I'll have you escorted out," Eleanor says.

184

Silent as a cat, a beefy man in a suit with an earpiece slinks through the doorway, a wooden expression on his face.

I flinch at the sight of him. So that's who the second vehicle belongs to.

I turn back to Eleanor. "Are you threatening me?"

"I'm advising you to be careful. You made unsubstantiated allegations about my son. He may be dead, but I won't let you slander him."

"He was a serial cheater and a pervert."

"Says the criminal with a record."

"He stalked women. I saw the photos."

Eleanor tinkles a scornful laugh. "What photos?"

"Callie told me you took them. You've probably destroyed them by now. But I have backups."

"Meaningless," she scoffs. "If anything, they indicate your intention to blackmail our family with fabricated claims."

My heart is racing so hard it feels like it's coming up my throat. Could Eleanor be sending those Facebook messages to scare me off? I won't be intimidated by her wealth or power. And I won't let her and Theo destroy Callie either. I need to get her out from under their control before they break her and she confesses to everything.

If that happens, I'll be going to prison with her. It's a price I'm not willing to pay.

CHAPTER 59

After leaving Callie's house, I speed all the way to Marco's place, my heart thudding wildly in my chest. He opens the door to me in baggy sweats and a threadbare T-shirt, clutching the oversized *Computer Whisperer* mug that I bought him for his birthday. What little hair he's still holding on to is splayed in every direction. I'm guessing he just fell out of bed.

He turns around wordlessly and heads back inside, leaving the door wide open for me. It's not exactly a warm reception, but after being kicked out of Callie's house, it's all the invitation I need.

He plunks himself down in a chair and yawns loudly. "I assume you're here to tell me what no-good business you and your sister were up to in the middle of nowhere last night."

"I didn't want to argue with you in front of Callie." I pull up the Facebook message on my phone and hand it to him. "This is what it was about."

"*Silence is costly*," he reads. "*Bring an envelope with $5,000 cash at midnight.*" He looks up sharply and hands me back my phone. "Are you serious? You did what they asked?"

"Not exactly," I answer sheepishly. "We left an empty envelope."

Marco rubs a hand over his unshaven jaw. "Even stupider. You could have been killed. You've no idea what kind of nutcase you might be dealing with."

It's on the tip of my tongue to tell him we brought a gun along for protection, but that might not be the best idea while he's venting. It seems like everything I say is just adding fuel to the fire.

"Did you see who picked up the envelope?" Marco asks.

"No. Callie and I were hiding nearby but no one showed. We waited until we were half frozen before we called you."

Marco slurps his coffee, peering at me over the rim. "Do you think this is a serious threat, or just someone yanking your chain — trying to scare you, perhaps?"

"I don't know what the motive is, but I think I know who's behind it. I went to Callie's house this morning and Eleanor answered the door. When I asked to speak with Callie, she said Theo had taken her to their house and that she didn't want anything more to do with me."

"That doesn't sound right," Marco chimes in. "You two have been joined at the hip for the past couple of weeks."

"Right. The thing is," I go on, "Callie's not answering my texts or taking my calls anymore. Eleanor made it clear they don't want me anywhere near her. She accused me of manipulating Callie and slandering Lincoln. And she even hinted that I might be trying to use the photos proving Lincoln was a stalker to blackmail them. It's possible she was behind those Facebook messages, trying to scare me into silence. That's the only explanation I can come up with."

Marco looks perturbed. "If you're right, she's engaging in criminal behavior."

"I dread to think what she threatened Callie with to get her to comply," I say. "She was livid that I made that Facebook page to help find Athena."

"Seems like an odd reaction from someone whose granddaughter went missing."

"Unless she had something to do with it," I say.

Marco's brows shoot up. "Why on earth would she abduct her own granddaughter?"

I shrug. "It doesn't make any sense. But now that she's as good as abducted Callie, it makes me wonder. What if Callie was right all along about Lincoln having something to do with his daughter's disappearance? Eleanor might be covering for him. I'm beginning to suspect she knows more about Athena's disappearance than she's admitting to."

"Do you think she took Callie's phone from her?" Marco asks.

"I don't know, but I don't trust Eleanor Bramston. She could have drugged Callie for all I know."

"If she refuses to let you see your sister, you can ask for a welfare check," Marco says. "Call Detective Altman and see what he has to say about it. He's investigating your sister's husband's death. Eleanor can't stop him from talking to her."

I nod. "Good idea. I'll drive to the Bramston's house first and ask to speak to Callie. If they shut me down, I'll call Altman."

Marco drains the rest of his coffee. "Give me a few minutes to shower up and I'll go with you."

"You don't have to do that. I'm sure you've got plenty of work you need to do."

"It can wait. I don't like the idea of you going alone."

While Marco takes a shower, I clean up the kitchen and empty the dishwasher. I'm putting away the last of the silverware when my phone rings. My heart leaps when the unknown number comes up. I hurriedly slide my finger across the screen. "Hello, this is Piper."

"It's Michaela," a subdued voice says. "Are you . . . alone?"

"Yes," I say a tad breathlessly. "You said you have information for me. Do you know where Athena is?"

"No. But something was bothering her right before she disappeared. She wanted to tell me, but she couldn't. She was too scared of what might happen."

"What did she think was going to happen?"

There's an elongated moment of silence before Michaela responds. "She said her grandmother would kill her."

CHAPTER 60

Shock renders me speechless. Did I just hear what I thought I heard? Eleanor strikes me as a cold-hearted woman, but is she capable of killing her own flesh and blood? Like a typical teenager, Athena might have been exaggerating the situation.

"Do you have any idea what would make her grand-mother want to kill her?" I ask. "Was it something she over-heard, or did, or found out about?"

"No idea. But whatever it was, it must have been some-thing that threatened the Bramston family's reputation. That's what matters most to Eleanor."

My mind goes straight to the stalking photos. Is it possi-ble Athena discovered them? Or did she find out Lincoln was having an affair?

"You know Athena well," I say. "Do you think she found out something about her father?"

"Like what?" Michaela asks, sounding confused.

I grimace. I don't want to put words in her mouth, but I need to know if she's heard any rumors. "There's been talk about him and other women."

"Athena never mentioned anything about it to me. I know her dad and stepmom argued a lot."

"What did they argue about?"

189

"Money — mostly money, I think." Michaela sniffs. "Do you think her disappearance has anything to do with her father's death?"

"I don't know how the two could be connected," I say in a measured tone.

"It's just weird, isn't it?" Michaela goes on. "They're saying he killed himself. That doesn't sound like Mr. Bramston."

The hair on the back of my neck stands up. "Guilt can make people do strange things," I say. "Maybe he had something to do with Athena's disappearance."

"No way," Michaela says. "Athena adores her dad, and he adored her. Her stepmom though . . ." Her voice trails off as though she's suddenly remembered that I'm Callie's sister.

"It's okay," I say with a chuckle. "Don't hold back on my account. I know she's entitled and spoiled."

"It's just that Athena badly wanted a little brother or sister, but Callie didn't want kids," Michaela says. "All she really seemed to care about were her salon appointments and endless shopping trips."

I grip the phone tighter, thinking back to my conversation with Callie about Lincoln's vasectomy. She made it sound like she was the one who wanted kids, and he had denied her. But from what I know of Callie, a kid would be an inconvenient addition to her lifestyle. Was she lying to me, or did Athena make things up to get attention?

"I need to get back to class," Michaela says. "I'm sorry I couldn't be more helpful."

"You've been very helpful," I assure her. "I really appreciate you reaching out."

"You won't mention my name to Athena's grandmother, will you?"

"No, you have my word. I share your apprehension about going up against that woman."

Michaela gives a nervous chuckle. "I hope you get to meet Athena soon. She'd love to have an aunt like you. I think you two would get along well."

Tears unexpectedly prickle my eyes. I've only just found my family and they're being snatched from me faster than I can get to know them. "I hope so too," I manage to choke out before Michaela ends the call.

Marco reappears, dressed in clean jeans and a long-sleeved shirt. I can't remember the last time I saw him looking this sharp. He must be expecting Eleanor to invite us in.

"Michaela finally called me back," I tell him. "She said Athena was worried about something before she disappeared. She thinks it had to do with the Bramston family — something that would have angered her grandmother if it had got out. Athena said her grandmother would kill her if she told anyone."

Marco lets out a long low whistle. "Any idea what it was?"

I hesitate for only a moment. "My guess is that she found out her father was stalking women."

CHAPTER 61

When we pull up at the Bramston residence a short time later, I'm not surprised to see a gated entry. The driveway up to the house is so long, I can't see from here if there are any cars parked outside. Not likely. They have at least a five-car garage, if the opulence of the gates is anything to go by.

I steel myself for a fight as I put the car in park. I'm not looking forward to a faceless confrontation via intercom, but if that's what it comes down to, I'm fully resolved to coming out victorious.

Marco glances over at me. "I take it you don't know the code."

"No." I roll down the window. "Trust me, they'll let us in after they hear what I have to say."

I buzz the intercom and tap my fingers impatiently on the steering wheel while I wait for someone to respond. I have to stay focused on Callie and why she won't, or can't, communicate with me. I'm worried Eleanor and Theo might have threatened her or even drugged her.

A female voice I don't recognize comes over the intercom. "Can I help you?"

I tilt my chin up for the benefit of any cameras. "I'm here to see Callie Bramston. I'm her sister, Piper Madden."

"One moment, please."

One moment stretches into five, and I press the intercom again. I'm not going to sit here forever like I'm waiting for an audience with royalty. Another minute or two goes by before the stranger's voice comes back over the intercom. "Callie Bramston is unavailable. Can I take a message?"

"I'm afraid that's unacceptable. I'm her sister and I demand to see her. I'm concerned about her welfare and I'm willing to notify the authorities to meet me here, if need be, as well as the media, to make sure they catch it all on camera."

Silence meets me on the other end. Just as I'm about to start ramming the intercom button in frustration, the gates begin to creep open. I smirk to myself as I put the car in gear. The last thing the Bramston matriarch wants is a bevy of cops and news crews swarming her gate.

"This is an impressive piece of property," Marco mutters, as we cruise up the sweeping tree-lined driveway.

"Trust me, the better they look on the outside, the darker the secrets they're hiding."

He shoots me a loaded look. "Let's hope they're not as dark as you're projecting."

I pull up outside the colonial-style mansion behind Callie's Tesla and turn off the ignition. This place looks like a more elaborate version of Callie's house. The Bramstons must employ a team of gardeners to manage the expansive grounds. I can't imagine what it costs to run this property. No wonder Eleanor is ruthless when it comes to preserving her family's power and image. There's a lot at stake.

"You'd better wait in the car," I say to Marco.

"And let you walk alone into the Colosseum to be mauled to death? I don't think so." He clambers out of the car before I can stop him and slams the door.

"Suit yourself," I say.

I ring the doorbell and step back as it cycles through its pretentious chime.

A maid appears and ushers us through to a sitting room. "Mrs. Bramston will be with you shortly." She slips out of the room before I have a chance to ask her which Mrs. Bramston she's referring to.

I don't have to wait long to find out. I hear the click of her heels first, and then the cold front of her presence sweeps into the room.

CHAPTER 62

Eleanor Bramston's glacial gaze lands on Marco first. "And you are?"

"Marco Diaz," he replies, jumping up and extending a hand.

Eleanor ignores the gesture as she takes a seat. "I thought as much. Faulkner told me Piper's little friend was some kind of computer hacker."

Marco grins. "I'll take that as a compliment. I'm a cyber security expert. I get paid to expose vulnerabilities in network infrastructures."

"I don't appreciate you showing up here uninvited." Eleanor turns to me, ratcheting her glare up a notch. "And I especially don't appreciate your threats at the gate. The security tapes will be passed along to my legal team for review."

"It sounds to me as if you're the one issuing threats," I say.

"Let me make it clearer. You're harassing our family at a particularly traumatic time in our lives. Callie has had more than enough of your interference and manipulation. You've been playing on her emotions — pretending you're getting Facebook messages and blackmail threats and dragging her out on a pointless stakeout where she almost died of hypothermia. Her ankles are so badly blistered they're at risk of becoming infected."

A pang of guilt hits at the mention of Callie's feet. I shouldn't have made her start walking back. She was definitely limping by the time Marco swooped in and rescued us.

"I'm sure we can both agree she's unlikely to die of sepsis from a few blisters," I say. "If you refuse to let me see her, I'll have no choice but to follow through on my 'threat,' as you called it, to initiate a welfare check." I pause for effect. "Some of us are genuinely concerned when our relatives go missing."

Eleanor narrows her eyes at me. "How dare you insinuate I don't care about my own flesh and blood! I've forked out a small fortune in private services trying to locate my runaway granddaughter while the police do nothing."

"Maybe that's the problem. As long as the cops think she's a runaway, they're going to keep looking in all the wrong places."

Marco clears his throat. "Piper, perhaps—"

"And where would you suggest we look?" Eleanor cuts in.

I keep my expression impassive. "Maybe she's closer to home than everyone thinks."

Eleanor gets to her feet, scowling. "I've listened to enough of your slanderous garbage. I suggest you and your hacker sidekick leave quietly before I call security to escort you out."

Marco raises his hands in a placating gesture. "No need for that. We'll leave of our own accord."

"And then we'll camp out at your gate and let the media interview us," I add.

Eleanor sets her lips in a tight line. "Very well. If you won't take my word for it, you can listen to some hard truths from your sister directly."

The minute she swooshes out of the room, Marco turns to me. "Don't stir things up. You can't win with someone like Eleanor Bramston."

"I'm not going to lie down and let that bully steamroll over me. I said I would be there for my sister, and I intend to keep my promise, no matter the cost."

Marco throws me a knowing look, but wisely says nothing. We can't be sure we're not being recorded.

Footsteps approach, and a moment later, Callie appears in the doorway, shadowed by Eleanor.

"Callie!" I jump to my feet and rush over to hug her, but she stands there stiffly as though I'm contaminated.

"Are you okay?" I ask, releasing her thin frame.

"Of course she's not okay," Eleanor chips in. She takes her by the elbow and guides her over to the couch. A shiver runs down my spine. It's almost as though my sister has been body snatched and replaced by a lobotomized version of herself.

I grimace when I see how slowly she's moving. She's wearing fuzzy slippers, and the backs of her heels are heavily bandaged. I'm not sure if it's for attention, or if she's really in that much pain. She slumps down in a chair, squeezing her hands in her lap, head hung forward.

Eleanor leans over and pats Callie's hands. "Tell your sister what you need her to hear."

She says nothing, her limp hair an unwashed curtain shielding her from scrutiny. Fear squeezes like a fist around my heart. What have they done to my sister? Is she hiding bruises?

I perch on the edge of my chair, locking my gaze on her in a bid to convey support. If she wants out of here, I'll take her with me right now with nothing but her slippers and the clothes on her back. I don't have much to offer her, but we'll figure something out.

"Callie," I blurt out, "you can come home with me if you don't want to stay here. You don't have to be afraid. There's nothing they can do to hurt you."

After a lengthy silence, she lifts her head, a vacant look in her eyes. "It's not them I'm afraid of, it's you."

CHAPTER 63

I feel like I'm frozen in time with a dagger wedged in my gut. I can't move my limbs, can't speak, can't even compute what my sister just said. After everything I've done for her, and everything we've been through together over the past few days, how can she possibly say she's afraid of me? Does she even know who I am?

Willing myself into motion, I sink to my knees in front of her and take her hands in mine. "Callie, it's me, Piper. Your sister."

I smile tentatively at her, but she snatches her hands away and blinks blankly at me.

"Callie, please say something!" I beg.

Eleanor clears her throat, a triumphant gleam in her eye. "Clearly, she has nothing more to say to you."

"What have you done to her?" I cry. "Have you given her something?"

Eleanor shakes her head in an exaggerated show of exasperation. "The only thing that's been done to her is the pain you inflicted on her. Now, if you don't leave the premises voluntarily, I will have you cited for trespassing."

"Callie," I say in an imploring tone. "I know this isn't really what you want. You need to speak up if you want to come with me."

She clenches her fists and tilts her trembling chin up. "Please . . . leave."

Marco lays a hand on my shoulder. I didn't even hear him walking over. "Let's go, Piper."

Defeated, I get to my feet. I feel like I'm in the twilight zone. I know this isn't what Callie wants. Not after everything she's been through with this family, and everything she's told me about them, and certainly not after everything she found out about her husband. That knowledge has put her in danger. I'm terrified she's going to disappear now too. Eleanor Bramston could tell everyone she took an extended trip to Europe to grieve, and no one would even question it.

In a daze, I follow the maid, who appears out of nowhere to escort us back to the front door. This time it's Marco steering me by the elbow. I feel a flicker of anger rising inside me. What is it about this house that turns people into institutionalized wrecks?

"I'll drive," Marco says, holding his hand out for the key. "You're shaking like a leaf."

I close my fingers into a fist. "No! I won't let them see me defeated. Callie may be too weak to stand up to them, but I'll find a way to get her out of there."

I start the engine and peel out of the driveway, spewing gravel with my tires.

Marco braces himself on the dash. "Hey! Slow down! I don't know what you think you can do, Piper, but you're not some kind of superhero just because you survived a few months behind bars. Callie's a grown woman. If she wants to be with her in-laws at a time like this, it's her choice. Maybe it's important to her to be with people who knew her husband."

"Are you kidding me? He cheated on her and lied to her about it. He was a pervert who stalked women. He controlled all their money and abused her. The last thing she wants is to be around the people who tried to protect him from the consequences of his actions."

"She's obviously in shock — it's probably just hitting her now that she killed him," Marco says.

I glare at him. "She didn't kill him. It was an accident."

He runs a hand over his head. "It doesn't change the fact that he died at her hands. And you helped her cover it up, so now she has to keep that guilt bottled up inside her."

"She can talk about it with me," I shoot back.

"Apparently, she doesn't want to." He shakes his head slowly. "You made a big mistake not coming clean about what she did. They're going to squeeze the truth out of her, sooner or later. You need to think long and hard about what you're going to do about that."

CHAPTER 64

I sleep fitfully, troubled by distorted dreams where Callie is locked in a soundproofed room somewhere on the Bramston estate, her mascara-streaked cheeks glistening with tears as she bangs on the padded door crying out my name. Each time I wake with a jolt, drenched with sweat and more determined than ever to rescue her.

Marco's words haunt me as I drive to work the following morning. *You need to think long and hard about what you're going to do about that.*

Short of staging some kind of intervention, I'm not sure there's a whole lot I can do. If Callie has chosen to align herself with Eleanor, for whatever reason, asking for a welfare check will be useless.

I wish I could stay home today too and concentrate on figuring out what to do to get Callie out from Eleanor's clutches. But Jenna has been more than generous already. I can't let her down again.

"Well, did your lead pan out?" she asks when I walk into the back room, where she's busy rolling out pastry.

I grimace as I pull my hair into a ponytail. "It's complicated. It turned out to be a friend of Athena's — her name's

Michaela. She told me something was bothering Athena before she disappeared. She was terrified of what her grandmother would do if she found out. It jives with everything I've learned about Eleanor Bramston. She intimidates everyone she meets."

Jenna frowns as she scrapes batter out of a mixing bowl. "She certainly has that reputation."

"What's worse is that Callie is staying with Eleanor and Theo now. Somehow, they've managed to convince her that I'm a threat to her wellbeing. I don't know what they're holding over her head, or if they're drugging her with something, but I'm afraid for her. I went to Eleanor and Theo's house yesterday and insisted on speaking with her. She was like a zombie. I offered to take her with me, but she refused to leave. It doesn't make any sense, because she can't stand them."

"Call Detective Altman," Jenna suggests, placing a hand on her hip. "Request a welfare check."

"It won't accomplish anything if Callie won't speak up. They're holding something over her head. I'm afraid she might disappear too, just like Athena."

Jenna's eyes widen. "You don't think Eleanor Bramston would harm her, do you?"

"At this point, I'm not ruling anything out," I reply, tying an apron around my waist. "There's something seriously wrong with that family."

* * *

By 9:00 a.m. the Wicked Scone is bustling with customers, and for a while I manage to forget about Callie and Athena and how complicated my life has become since Marco inadvertently helped me find my sister.

I'm in the middle of taping up a box of assorted pastries for one of our regular customers when I look up to see Detective Altman striding through the door accompanied by several officers. His expression is inscrutable as he marches over to me.

"Piper Madden, you're under arrest."

CHAPTER 65

I feel myself moving through a sea of familiar and unfamiliar faces laced with equal measures of horror and disbelief. Awestruck children clutch their parent's hands tightly as I'm marched past them in handcuffs, still wearing my pink Wicked Scone apron and sporting the scent of sugar and freshly baked bread. I don't remember being read my Miranda rights or even the moment I was handcuffed. I think I must have zoned out after I heard I was being arrested.

As I walk out the door, I catch a glimpse of Jenna standing off to the side in her floury apron, a distraught expression on her face.

"I'm sorry," I mouth to her.

Her eyes widen and I realize she's misconstrued my apology as an admission of guilt. But there's no time to correct the misunderstanding as I'm whisked out the door.

A crowd has assembled on the sidewalk and watches unapologetically as an officer bundles me into the back of a squad car. I stare miserably through the window at the idling spectators as I listen to Detective Altman communicate with dispatch. A sense of gloom descends over me. It feels like déjà vu, only this time I'm in even more dire straits than before.

I'm facing my worst fears. Callie must have confessed to everything. I should have heeded Marco's warning. It didn't take long for the Bramston matriarch to break her down.

I breathe out a sigh of relief when Altman finally finishes conversing on his radio and puts the car in gear. I've had enough of the sea of eyes boring into me like frogspawn. None of them are well-wishers, they're all there for the show.

"Why am I under arrest?" I ask, trying to quell the quiver in my voice.

"We'll discuss that at the station. Just sit back and enjoy the ride for now," Altman replies.

"Is that meant to be a joke? You literally just arrested me at work in front of my boss and all my customers."

"It will be a lot easier if you take a deep breath and sit tight until we get there."

I sink back against the seat and close my eyes. I need to think. I should have taken Marco's advice and sorted out some legal counsel before I actually needed to call on them. Speaking of calls, I wonder if they'll let me make one when I get to the station. The problem is, I don't know any lawyers, so I'm going to have to lean on Marco once again. I'm pretty sure I've exhausted the goodness of his heart, and he's only helping me out of obligation at this point. But I'm too desperate to be proud.

I'm curious if Callie has been arrested too, but it's not as if Altman's going to give me that information. They'll keep us separated in the hope we trip ourselves up on a lie. I groan inwardly. If Callie has already told the cops everything, there's no way I'm getting out of this. I'm not familiar with the intricacies of the law, but I'm pretty sure I'm in line for a slew of charges — abuse of a corpse, if nothing else. There's probably a technical term for covering up a crime too. Knowing my luck, the list of charges will grow over the next few days. My criminal history won't do me any favors. I wonder if a lawyer can have that ruled inadmissible.

When we reach the station, Altman opens the back door of the squad car and helps me out. Unlike at the bakery, no one pays me much attention as I'm led inside. I'm booked, searched, and fingerprinted, then left in a holding cell while Altman inventories my personal items and completes the necessary paperwork related to my arrest. I'm unsure what happens next. Will they keep me here tonight, or send me to jail? Best case scenario they'll take my statement, give me a court date, and release me. But I'm not holding my breath. "I want to speak to a lawyer," I tell Altman when he returns.

He nods and retrieves my phone.

I dial Marco's number and scrunch my eyes shut while it rings.

"I need your help," I mutter when he answers.

"Car trouble?"

"I've been arrested."

CHAPTER 66

"I need a lawyer, Marco," I say. "I hate to ask for another favor, but I don't know who else to call. I would have called Callie but, under the circumstances . . ." I trail off, unsure if I should say any more within earshot of officers walking by.

"I'll handle it," he replies in a measured tone, giving me some assurance that I'm not alone and helpless in this mess.

True to his word, a young, smartly dressed, bespectacled lawyer appears at my cell door within the hour and introduces himself as Barry Pearson. I'm relieved to see him but conflicted as to how much to reveal.

"Marco Diaz retained me to represent you," he says. "Give me a couple of minutes and I'll arrange for us to talk in private."

A short time later, an officer escorts us to an interview room. Seated in a plastic chair opposite my lawyer, it hits me that I'm depending on this man's competence to spare me the fate of spending the best years of my life in prison for a rash decision I made for a sister I barely know.

"Looks like you're being charged with obstruction of justice in the investigation into your brother-in-law's murder," Barry says, shuffling through some papers. "The prosecutor might elect to pursue additional charges once they hear the evidence."

"I didn't kill him," I say quietly.

Barry scrutinizes me for a moment, then nods. "I believe you."

"Can you get me out of here? Can I post bail or something?"

"We'll get to that," he says, adjusting the sleeve of his expensive suit jacket. "Why don't we start at the beginning? How did you get involved with the Bramstons?"

"Marco gifted me a subscription to myancestry.com. I discovered I had a biological sister I knew nothing about. Turns out we were both adopted at birth. She married Lincoln Bramston. I didn't really know him. I only met him a couple of times."

"What was your impression of him?"

I let out a snort. "He barely said two words to me. Just enough to make it clear I wasn't welcome in his house."

Barry jots down a few notes as I talk. "How did your sister and Lincoln get along?"

"Not well. They argued the night he died."

"About what?"

"About me, and about the fact that he was a serial cheater. Callie thinks he was having an affair with their next-door neighbor, Vanessa Ridley. He denied it, of course."

Barry hefts an eyebrow. "Is there any evidence of this alleged affair?"

"Callie walked in on several private conversations between them. And she found a birthday card Lincoln had hidden that said something like 'I can't wait until we can be together.' It was signed 'your X factor.'"

"Where is this card?"

"She put it in the safe. If her in-laws get their hands on it, they'll destroy it, just like they did with the surveillance photos."

Barry wrinkles his brow. "What surveillance photos are you referring to?"

"Lincoln was stalking women. Callie found dozens of photos of different women hidden in a folder in his closet. I have copies of some of them on my phone. It's obvious none of the women knew they were being photographed. Pretty creepy, if you ask me. He was leading a double life the whole time. Maybe that's why he was killed."

Barry twists his pen between his fingers. "It certainly widens the suspect pool. Let's get back to the night Lincoln died. What were you doing at the house?"

"Having dinner with my sister. We've been hanging out a lot — making up for lost time. Callie began to open up to me. She told me Lincoln was abusive, and she wanted out of the marriage, but she had to be careful how she went about it. The Bramstons are a powerful family."

Barry sets down his pen and looks squarely at me. "How did you feel knowing your sister was stuck in an abusive marriage?"

The hairs on the back of my neck prickle. "I felt bad for her, of course."

Barry scratches his jaw. "The coroner's report concludes that Lincoln Bramston was dead before he went into the ravine. I need you to be honest with me, Piper. Did your sister have anything to do with her husband's death?"

CHAPTER 67

"Of course she didn't have anything to do with his death," I say. "She's devastated, even though he was a jerk to her. I don't understand why I'm being charged with obstruction of justice. I've cooperated fully with the investigation."

Barry sighs and flicks through a folder on the desk in front of him before pulling out a sheet of paper. He slides it across the table to me and taps a finger on it. "The DNA results of the hairs found in the vehicle match the sample you gave to Detective Altman."

My mouth drops open. How can that be? I was careful to put my hair inside that baseball cap, and I even placed a sheet over the seat before I got in. My mind spins faster than a dryer as I try to collect my thoughts. It must have happened when we were struggling to get Lincoln's body into the driver's seat. My heart sinks. If they have DNA evidence against me, it changes everything.

I give a nonchalant shrug. "I don't know how it got in the car but it's hardly surprising. I've spent a lot of time with my sister at her house over the past few days. It's entirely possible some hair got transferred on some clothing and ended up in one of their vehicles."

"It's true it's circumstantial evidence." Barry frowns. "But I understand that's not the only evidence they have against you. I'm waiting on copies of the full forensic analysis and also copies of statements made by your sister and her in-laws. We'll know more then."

"My sister will back me up," I say, exuding more confidence than I feel inside. "Her in-laws' statements are worthless. They'll lie through their teeth to protect Lincoln's reputation, even in death. They stole the surveillance photos Callie found and destroyed them. I wouldn't be surprised if Eleanor Bramston had something to do with her granddaughter's disappearance. Athena might have discovered what her father was up to."

Barry pushes his glasses up his nose. He's got a bit of a Clark Kent look about him. I only hope he has the superpowers to go with it. I'm going to need them to get out of this mess.

"Don't get sidetracked worrying about Athena right now," Barry says. "You need to stay focused on your own situation."

"She's my niece. Someone needs to worry about her now that she's lost her father."

"First things first," Barry goes on. "There's nothing you can do to help her as long as you're locked up in here."

"So, can you get me out?"

"Not until after the arraignment. It's a circumstantial case and you're not a flight risk or anything, but it's a serious charge and you do have a criminal history, so that will work against you. I'm going to give it my best shot. But I can't make any promises."

"When's the arraignment?" I ask, with a growing sense of dread that I'm going to be stuck in jail for weeks — possibly months.

"Tomorrow morning. I'm afraid you've got to get through a night in jail first."

My stomach twists at the thought. I never in a million years expected to be back in this position. Has Callie been locked up too? She'll never last a night without her

Egyptian-cotton sheets. Eleanor's highfalutin legal team will likely manage to have her declared unfit to stand trial, and they'll take her to a psychiatric facility instead. Not that it would be a whole lot better than prison.

"Can I make a call to Marco?" I ask. "I need to let him know I'm all right."

Barry slides his phone across to me. "Go ahead."

I dial Marco's number, praying he'll answer. He's already done everything he can to help me and more, but I need to hear his voice, and feel his strength, on the other end of the line.

"Hey, Barry," Marco says.

"It's me," I squeak out, trying not to dissolve into tears.

"Piper! Are you out?" he asks, a thread of hope in his voice.

"No, I'm still at the station. I'm being transferred to jail until the arraignment tomorrow. They've got DNA evidence against me. They're claiming the hairs they found in the vehicle match mine. Barry's going to do his best to get me out on bail."

"If there's a way to make it happen, he'll get it done. He's good at his job," Marco says.

"I know. I just wanted to call and say thank you for everything. I can't tell you how grateful I am to have a lawyer who knows what he's doing."

"You'll get through this, Piper. You're strong. I'll be at the arraignment tomorrow to support you."

"Thanks," I sniffle.

I hang up and hand the phone back to Barry.

He slips it into his jacket pocket and gets to his feet. "I'll be in touch. Keep your chin up."

I give a wry smile. "I'll be fine. It's not my first rodeo."

He exits the room, leaving me alone with my thoughts. I sink my head into my hands, my shoulders shaking. I can stay strong on the outside but inside this is tearing me up. How could I have been careless enough to leave my DNA in the Mercedes?

And then it hits me.

211

CHAPTER 68

Lying prostrate on my thin, vinyl mattress in the small jail cell I've been condemned to for the night, I study a crack in the corner of the wall. In my mind, I'm replaying the same scene over and over again — me telling Callie to comb her hair so she wouldn't look like a mad woman in the event we were pulled over. She acted like she didn't have a hairbrush in her enormous purse. I remember handing her mine, but I was focused on more important things than watching her brush out her matted hair. She could easily have pocketed a few hairs, and I would have been none the wiser.

I desperately want to give her the benefit of the doubt. It's possible I accidentally transferred a few strands of my hair while we were wrestling Lincoln's body into the driver's seat. But I can't ignore the possibility that she deliberately placed those hairs in the car. Did she set me up to take the fall in case things didn't go according to plan? Would she betray me like that? The truth is, I don't know. I don't know who the real Callie is — the uber-confident woman I met in Starbucks, or the frightened, zombified version I spoke to at the Bramston residence. Or is she both — an incredibly good actress who can morph into whatever the situation calls for?

* * *

By the time I arrive at the courthouse the following morning, I'm no clearer on whether my sister betrayed me. I look around the room, hoping to spot her, but she's nowhere in sight. I catch a glimpse of Marco and give him a tentative smile.

Barry leans over and whispers, "We got the best possible judge we could for the arraignment. I've worked with Nelson a lot in the past; he's a reasonable man."

Despite his reassurance, I'm not allowing myself to get my hopes up. The disappointment would be too soul crushing.

I zone out once the proceedings get underway and the back-and-forth legalese begins. My mind drifts to Jenna and the Wicked Scone. I can't help wondering what my regulars are saying about me. I can only imagine the gossip being exchanged over a Danish pastry or a cranberry scone.

Before I know it, the arraignment is over, and Barry is pumping my hand.

"Wh-what happened?" I ask blinking in bewilderment.

He chuckles. "Congratulations! You made bail."

"Thank you," I gasp. "I can't believe it."

Marco appears at my side, and I fall into his arms, sobbing. "I'll never be able to repay you for this."

"You already have," he says. "Come on, let's get out of here."

"Call the office and make an appointment to see me tomorrow," Barry says, reaching for his briefcase.

Marco takes me to lunch in an upscale bistro to celebrate. "Here's to Barry," he says, clinking his water glass to mine.

"I can't imagine what he's costing you," I say.

"Don't worry about the money."

"I can't help it. You worked hard for it. It's not as if you're a Bramston with a trust fund and a string of hotels to your name."

"Not yet," he says with a smirk.

The waiter arrives at our booth with a tray of food, and I let out a moan of pleasure at the sight of the juice dripping from my Swiss mushroom burger.

"This looks galaxies better than what I ate in prison yesterday," I whisper as the waiter glides out of earshot.

"What's Barry's plan going forward?" Marco asks.

I bite into a Parmesan fry and swallow it. "He's waiting for copies of statements from Callie and her in-laws." I take a sip of my water and lock eyes with him. "I think I've figured out how my hair ended up in the Mercedes."

He raises a brow. "How?"

"The night Lincoln died, Callie asked to borrow my hairbrush. It could have been an accidental transfer. But—"

"It could have been deliberate," Marco finishes for me. He drops his burger onto his plate and leans back in his chair, smoothing a hand over the top of his glistening head. "That witch set you up."

"If she did, it was only because she panicked. I talked her into covering up what happened. She didn't want to go to prison if we were caught."

Marco shoots me an incredulous look. "You don't get it, do you? It wasn't a spur-of-the-moment thing that night. She set you up from the very beginning to take the fall for Lincoln's murder."

CHAPTER 69

"What are you talking about?" I ask. "She didn't mean to kill Lincoln. It was an accident. They were arguing about the photos. He threw her against the wall — she shoved him back and he fell down the stairs."

Marco sets his jaw in a grim line. "So she says." He sweeps a glance around the restaurant, then leans across the table to me. "Don't you find it a little odd that you told your sister what you went to prison for, and then her husband ends up dying in the exact same manner a couple of days later?"

I reach for another fry and stab it absentmindedly into the pool of ketchup on my plate. "I thought it was an unhappy coincidence. I knew it wouldn't look good for me if my criminal past came to light. But I never considered the fact that it could have been a set-up." It pains me even to say the words. Callie wasn't particularly endearing when we first met, but she's still my biological sister. I had high hopes we would form a bond, and I honestly believed she was warming up to me. The thought that she saw me only as a pawn in her plot to get rid of her husband is a hard pill to swallow.

"But why would she kill Lincoln?" I ask. "Revenge for his affairs?"

Marco shrugs. "Or money."

I chew on my lip as I consider the possibility. "I don't know. It seems a stretch to think she killed him for money. And she'd hardly kill him just because he was having an affair. It wasn't the first time he'd cheated on her, by all accounts. Maybe the stalking photos were a step too far. She could have flipped out in the moment."

"Let me see those photos," Marco says, gesturing for my phone.

I pull them up and show them to him.

He taps on the screen for a few minutes, then lets out a grunt. "Yep. Just what I thought."

"What?"

"I ran those pictures through Google Lens. They're all pulled from the web. Lincoln didn't take any of them."

My jaw drops. The sickening realization that I've been conned spreads through me like neurotoxin from a venomous bite. "Eleanor said she didn't know what I was talking about when I accused her of taking them," I say. "Callie must have destroyed them herself."

"And the photo of Emma you never got to see — I'm guessing it didn't exist," Marco adds.

I push my plate to one side, my appetite gone. How could Callie have pretended her husband was the creep who assaulted Emma? This is the biggest betrayal of all. I shared about the most vulnerable period of my life in the hope we would bond over something so tragic and personal. Instead, she took the information and used it against me.

I take a few shallow breaths, shaking with anger. I have no idea anymore where the truth begins and the lies end. "I'm beginning to think she made all that up about Lincoln being abusive and having a dark side too," I say. "If anything, he was frustrated with her manipulative ways. No wonder he was so angry when he saw me in the house. He might have thought she was scheming with me."

Marco sets his lips in a grim line. "I bet she made that up about him having an affair with the next-door neighbor too.

216

The card you found could have been from anyone. It might have been left behind by the previous owners."

I give a glum nod. "Vanessa denied the affair when I confronted her. I'm screwed, Marco. I can only imagine the lies Callie's told the police about me."

"All you can do now is tell them the truth. You should never have tried to cover up what she did, but you didn't kill the man."

"They're never going to believe me over her. She's aligned herself with her powerful in-laws."

Marco gives a disgusted grunt. "Or she's pretending to, now that she stands to inherit Lincoln's money."

I frown as another thought occurs to me. "If this was about inheriting his money, then it's awfully convenient his daughter's no longer in the picture."

CHAPTER 70

Marco stares across the table at me, a horror-stricken look on his face. "Are you suggesting what I think you're suggesting?"

I give a helpless shrug. "I don't know what Callie's capable of. All this time I thought Eleanor Bramston might have had something to do with her granddaughter's disappearance, but what if it was Callie? Athena's friend told me she never wanted kids. What if she was systematically getting rid of all the obstacles standing between her and Lincoln's money?"

Marco curls his fingers into a fist on the table. "If you're right, Eleanor and Theo Bramston are in danger too. Next thing you know, their house will burn down during the night or something equally coincidental."

"They'll never listen to me if I try and warn them," I say. "And the police will never believe it either. We need proof."

Marco squeezes his jaw. "You said Callie was staying with her in-laws. Is there anyone at her house?"

I shake my head. "She and Lincoln don't have live-in staff."

"What about a dog?"

I arch a scoffing brow. "Are you kidding me? Callie's too self-centered to care for anyone but herself."

Marco nods. "Good. We'll pay her place a visit. If I can get into her computer, I might find something incriminating, or something that will point us in the right direction at least. Her search history could be revealing for starters."

"How are we going to get into her house? I don't have the access code."

Marco grins. "That's the easy part. I can hack their app-based lock and deactivate the alarm system."

I throw him a dubious look. "From what I've seen, Vanessa and Doug next door keep a close eye on things. What if they spot us?"

"We won't hide from them. We'll go undercover instead. I'll borrow one of the vans from my buddy's plumbing business. Are you in?"

"I don't know. I don't want you risking everything for me."

The expression on his face softens. "The only risk I'm unwilling to take is the risk of losing you."

I open my mouth to say something, but the right words evade me.

Marco signals to our server for the check. "Let's get out of here. The sooner we jump on this, the better. There's no telling when Callie might return home."

* * *

My heart is floating up my throat by the time we arrive at Callie's house. Dressed in blue overalls, I pull my Jensen Plumbing cap low over my eyes and reach for a coil of hose-pipe in the back of the truck. Marco lifts out a heavy-duty tool bag and leads the way to the front door. We're inside in under a minute, which both impresses and scares me. Marco immediately gets to work deactivating the alarm system and the cameras.

My heart judders in my chest as I lead him down the hallway to Callie's den. If we're caught inside her house, no amount of explaining will get us out of this mess.

"Relax! You're twitching like a frightened rabbit. Everything's going to be all right," Marco assures me as he gets to work.

Within minutes, he's firing up the computer. "All right, let's take a deep dive into the world of Callie Bramston."

I sink down in a chair and leave him to work uninterrupted, glancing nervously over my shoulder from time to time, fearful I might spot Eleanor or Detective Altman darkening the doorway.

"Are you almost done?" I ask. "I have a bad feeling about this."

"I need a few more minutes. I installed some spyware and I'm just checking emails," he replies. "Callie drives a Tesla, right? Stupidly, she's saved her app login information in an email. That could be useful. I'll download the app on my phone. If she goes somewhere, we can follow her." He snaps a photo of the information with his phone, then resumes tapping on the keyboard.

I leap to my feet. "Can we go now, please? I don't want to be here too long in case Vanessa calls Callie to find out what her plumbing issue is."

Marco peers intently at the screen, seemingly oblivious to my request. "What did you say Vanessa's husband was called?"

"Doug. Doug Ridley. Why?"

Marco looks up at me, a gleam of satisfaction in his eye. "I think I know why Callie killed her husband."

CHAPTER 71

"We got it all wrong," Marco says. "Lincoln wasn't the one having an affair. It was Callie."

"What?" My jaw goes slack, shock ricocheting through my veins. "How do you know that? Let me see what you're looking at."

I peer over Marco's shoulder and scan the email on the screen.

Have you said anything to Lincoln? I need to know. You can't keep avoiding me. We need to talk. You know our love is real.

My gaze travels up to the sender: *Doug Ridley.*

An icy shiver runs down my spine. How could I have been such an idiot? Callie's been lying to me about everything. No wonder she seemed so shaken when I showed her the card I found in the attic — it was probably from Doug.

"I can't believe she managed to fool me," I say. "Do you think Lincoln knew?"

Marco grimaces. "I suspect he got wind of it — maybe that's why Callie killed him. I'm guessing the prenup had an infidelity clause. She would have walked away with nothing

221

if he'd divorced her. This way she gets everything." He hits print and hands me a copy of the email. "Keep this somewhere safe."

"I've just thought of something," I say, brushing a hand over my brow. "Doug might have been in on it. He might even have helped her kill Lincoln."

Marco powers down the computer and gets to his feet. "If he's been carrying on with Callie, he probably has the code to the house. Let's get out of here before he surprises us. I have access to her email account now, so I can go through the rest of it later."

"Should we tell Altman what we've found?" I ask.

Marco shoots me a cynical look. "We need to be a lot smarter than that. What we're doing is illegal."

He reaches for the tool bag at his feet, and we make our way back to the front door, where he resets the alarm. Outside, I throw a nervous glance around to check for any sign of Vanessa or Doug, before climbing back into the plumbing van.

My head is spinning as Marco peels out of the driveway. Everything I thought I knew about my sister has just been incinerated. If Lincoln found out about her affair, he might have confronted Doug. Could Doug have murdered him? Callie could have covered for him by pretending she was the one who pushed Lincoln down the stairs. And I was the fool who helped her stage a suicide.

"If Vanessa knows about the affair, or even suspects, she could be in danger too," I say. "It's only fair to warn her, but I'm not sure she'll listen to me."

"Callie is a lot more dangerous than any of us realized," Marco says. "You need to keep your distance. Ignore her if she asks to meet up with you. It won't be for any good reason."

We pull into Marco's driveway, and he switches off the engine. He turns to me, a pleading look in his eyes. "Promise me you won't try and contact Callie."

"It's not an option. I'm not allowed anywhere near any of the Bramstons. It's one of the conditions of my bail."

"Do you want to come in and wait while I go through her email account?" Marco asks.

"No, it's late. I should go. I have an 8:00 a.m. meeting with Barry in the morning, and I need to go to work after that."

"Are you sure that's a good idea?" Marco asks. "You're going to have to answer a lot of questions from your regulars. They won't hold back."

"I'll stay out in the prep area and let Jenna handle the customers. Keep me posted if you find anything else of interest in Callie's emails."

I climb into bed the minute I get home. I'm afraid I won't be able to fall asleep, but exhaustion gets the better of me and I drift off into unpleasant dreams of Callie's caustic laugh as I'm sentenced to life without parole.

* * *

I wake with a jolt the following morning, fearful I've overslept and am running late for work, but then I remember my meeting with Barry. A part of me dreads it because it makes this nightmare more real, but I'm thankful to have a competent lawyer on my side.

After going through the usual torturous process of trying to find something suitable to wear, I hurry out to my car clutching my travel mug of coffee.

Barry's assistant, Samantha, greets me from behind a sleek reception desk. I'm impressed that I can't see a spot of dust anywhere on the gleaming surface. It's as flawless as Samantha's skin, which I try not to be envious of.

"Barry will be right with you," she says, her smile another flash of perfection.

I'm flicking aimlessly through a magazine when he strides into view, tugging on his cuff sleeve. "Piper, good to see you. Please, come on through."

I toss the magazine back on the end table, then make a belated attempt to straighten it out, before following Barry into his office. Sinking down in a luxuriously comfortable leather chair, I take in the incredible view from the eighth-floor office occupied by Pearson & Weiss LLP.

"I really appreciate you getting me out on bail," I say. "What happens now?"

Barry leans back in his chair, tapping his pen on the desk in front of him. "I received a copy of Callie's statement late last night."

I roll my eyes. "What kind of lies is she telling about me?"

Barry sighs, tenting his fingers in front of him. "Did you steal your sister's gun?"

CHAPTER 72

I stare at Barry open-mouthed. "Did she tell you that?"

He shuffles a few pages on the desk in front of him. "It's in her statement. The police have obtained a search warrant for your apartment."

I groan and bury my face in my hands. "I didn't steal her gun. I put it in my purse because she was drunk, and I didn't think she should be anywhere near it. But I gave it back to her. I watched her lock it up in the safe."

Barry grimaces. "That's going to be a tough sell to a jury. She's claiming you stole it and never returned it."

"I'm telling you the truth. I didn't——"

He holds up a hand. "I believe you. Callie's also alleging you used the gun to threaten her."

"I never threatened her," I protest. "She was distraught about Lincoln's death. I took the gun from her because she was acting irrationally — waving it around and pointing it at me while holding a glass of wine in her other hand."

Barry raises his eyebrows. "Why did you put the gun in your purse and not in the safe to begin with? Were you planning on leaving with it?"

Panic flutters in my throat. I rack my brain for a response that sounds halfway plausible.

"If there's something you're keeping from me, now would be the time to tell me," Barry adds. "There's nothing to be gained from protecting your sister, because she's certainly not protecting you."

A cold thread of panic slithers through me. "What do you mean?"

Barry reaches for a sheet of paper in front of him. "According to her statement, you tried to convince her Lincoln was the man who assaulted your friend, Emma, in college."

I let out a disbelieving gasp. "That's a lie! She was the one who tried to convince me it was Lincoln. She told me he was at Cal State LA at the same time Emma was. She even told me she found a photo in his closet of a half-naked girl wearing Cal State LA sweatpants."

Barry pulls his notepad toward him and jots down a few things. "I'll have Samantha investigate it. It should be easy enough to confirm when and where Lincoln went to college."

"Are you saying she might have made that up too?"

Barry gives me a tight smile by way of response.

"What else did she say in her statement?" I ask, dreading his answer.

He focuses his attention back on the pages in front of him. "It says here, you told her what you did to the kid with the photo of Emma on his T-shirt. You said it was an easy way to disguise a murder, and you suggested doing the same thing to Lincoln. Callie admits she told you he was abusive, but she didn't want to kill him, just divorce him."

"So how does she explain him falling down the stairs?"

"According to her statement, you came over that night for dinner and insisted on staying until Lincoln came home. She was in the kitchen when she heard him scream. I'll read you her exact words: 'I came running out and found him at the bottom of the stairs. Piper was standing at the top, grinning. She told me that men who abuse women deserve what they get. I wanted to call the police right away, but she forced me at gunpoint to help her put my husband's body in the Mercedes.'"

I shake my head. "None of that is true."

Barry stabs his pen into his notepad and tosses it on the table. "Then what is the truth, Piper? Because I've been doing this long enough to know you're holding out on me."

CHAPTER 73

"As your lawyer, I want to remind you that anything you tell me is confidential," Barry says. "But it's going to be difficult for me to represent you adequately if all I have to build your defense on is half-truths."

I run my fingers through my hair, trying to sort through my tangled thoughts. If Callie set me up to take the fall, then all bets are off. I need to fight for my freedom, if it's not already too late.

"Truthfully," I begin, "I don't know what happened. I wasn't there, but I'm beginning to think it was no accident. Callie called me in tears that night and told me Lincoln was dead. I raced right over there. At first, she said she found him at the bottom of the stairs. When I pressed her, she admitted that they'd argued and she'd shoved him, but that it hadn't been intentional. She seemed genuinely distraught. She's my sister. I felt like I had no choice but to help her."

The expression on Barry's face hardens. "And exactly what type of help did you offer?"

My shoulders sag. "It was my suggestion to stage a suicide. I know it sounds like a dumb idea, but Callie had me convinced Lincoln was a sick individual and that his family would destroy her in the courts if she confessed to what she'd done. My only concern at that moment was to protect her. I couldn't bear the thought of her spending the rest of her life behind bars. I knew she wouldn't survive the ordeal — at least not the person she pretended to be."

Barry takes off his glasses and rubs his eyes. "Are you trying to tell me you put Lincoln's body in the Mercedes and pushed the car into the ravine?"

"Yes." My reply is barely audible even to myself.

Barry nods slowly as if to say he suspected as much. "Pretty convenient for Callie that only your DNA was found in the Mercedes."

"She put it there. She borrowed my hairbrush." I twiddle my fingers in my lap. "There's something else you should know."

Barry peers at me from behind his glasses. "What is it?"

"Callie was—"

My phone beeps and I sneak a glance at the incoming message from Marco.

I've found something.

My heart jackhammers in my chest.

"You were saying?" Barry prompts.

"Um . . . sorry. Someone's trying to get a hold of me. What I was saying is that I found out Callie was having an affair with her next-door neighbor, Doug Ridley."

Barry pulls his notepad toward him and starts scribbling. "How do you know that? Did she tell you?"

I let out a scoffing snort. "Hardly. She had me convinced it was Lincoln who was having an affair with Doug's wife, Vanessa."

Barry adjusts the sleeve of his jacket, fixing me with a skeptical gaze. "Do you have any evidence to back this up?"

"The card I told you about. Callie acted like she'd never seen it before, but I could tell she was shocked I had found it. I think it was from Doug."

Barry gives a disappointed grunt. "Unless he signed it, it doesn't prove anything."

"It suggests there was some kind of illicit relationship going on," I counter.

Barry makes a dismissive gesture with his hand. "We'll need better evidence than that — something that will hold up in court."

I unzip my purse and retrieve the email Marco printed out. "Will this suffice?" I ask, handing it to him.

He reads it through, then glances up at me. "Where did you get this from?"

"Callie's computer."

He tosses it on the table. "I'm assuming you accessed it without her permission. I won't ask how you managed to pull that off, but this is inadmissible."

"How can it be inadmissible? It proves my sister was having an affair with Doug Ridley. It gives her a motive to get rid of Lincoln."

Barry pushes his glasses up his nose. "If she set up Doug to make the kill, and you to take the fall, then her hands are clean."

CHAPTER 74

My mind is awash with chaotic thoughts as I leave Barry's office and drive to work. Jenna offered to let me take the day off, but I told her I needed the money and promised to stay in the prep room, out of sight and out of trouble.

When I arrive at the Wicked Scone, Jenna embraces me without a word.

"I know what everyone's saying, but I didn't kill my brother-in-law," I say when she releases me.

"I know you didn't." She lets out a heavy sigh. "I warned you the Bramston family was dangerous. You got sucked into their vortex of corruption."

I give her a weak smile. She doesn't know the half of it.

I get busy preparing a large batch of dough for our popular rosemary olive loaves. I'm going to miss serving the regulars today, like ninety-two-year-old Marge Simmons who comes in every day to buy a cheese Danish for her bedridden husband.

My phone rings and I glance at the screen to see Marco's name. "Hey," I say, reaching for a towel to dust off my hands. "What's up?"

"Are you alone?"

I throw a quick glance at the door. "Yes. I'm out back."

231

"I managed to hack into Callie's bank account. She's amassed a small fortune."

I frown. "She told me she didn't have any access to Lincoln's money. Eleanor cut her off."

"That may be, but Callie has quite the business empire of her own going. It appears your sister has been embezzling money from the Bramston family businesses overseas."

I sink down on a stool, trying to absorb the shock. "I can't believe it. Callie acted like she was clueless when it came to money. How on earth was she able to outsmart the Bramstons?"

"Exactly what I asked myself," Marco says. "That's when I decided to do a background check on Doug Ridley. Turns out he sells and trades corporate securities for a major invest-ment banking firm. Callie had expertise at hand, and a likely co-conspirator when it came to padding her pockets."

"So, it's possible Lincoln discovered what she was doing, and that's why she had to get rid of him," I say.

"That's what I'm thinking," Marco replies. "If he had found out about her affair with Doug, it wouldn't have been enough of a motive to kill him when she had so much money stashed away. On the other hand, if he had uncovered the financial fraud, she would have been looking at a lengthy prison sentence."

"How much money are we talking about?"

"A little over fourteen million dollars."

I whistle softly. It's a mind-boggling amount to someone who earns less than fourteen dollars an hour. "How on earth did she manage to siphon it without anyone noticing?"

"With Doug's expertise."

"I can't believe he would risk his career by committing financial fraud."

"It's not all that surprising. It happens every day."

My mind reels as I try to digest it. "All this time I sus-pected Lincoln had harmed his own daughter because she'd uncovered his double life," I say, thinking out loud. "But if Athena had found out about Callie and Doug, they might have gotten rid of her."

CHAPTER 75

"You have one twisted sister," Marco says. "And it's my fault your paths crossed."

"None of this is your fault."

"It's all my fault. That's why I'm going to do everything I can to help you get free of this nightmare."

"I'll be finished up at work soon," I say. "I'll come by your place afterward and we can talk then. Please don't do anything stupid."

* * *

When I pull up outside Marco's house, I'm relieved to see that the plumbing van has been returned to its rightful owner. It's one less thing to worry about in the event any of Callie's neighbors noticed it parked outside her house.

I've been fretting the whole way here that Marco might try something illegal, like holding Callie's money hostage and blackmailing her into telling the truth. I don't want him to lose his career over my mistakes.

"Hope you're hungry," he says, leading me into the kitchen. "I picked us up some Philly cheesesteak sandwiches."

I sit down at the table while he pours us each a glass of water.

"Thanks," I say, unwrapping my sandwich. "I'm starved. I skipped lunch today."

We eat in silence for a minute or two, then Marco says, "I think we have enough to go to the police. Financial fraud's a federal crime."

"But how are we going to explain how we got our hands on the information?"

"We'll turn it over to Barry. He can protect our anonymity." He wipes his mouth on a napkin. "I'm going to jump in the shower and then we can swing by his office. I left him a message already. He's there most evenings until eight or so."

He disappears out of the room, and I turn my attention back to my sandwich. My head jerks up when Marco's phone trills on the counter. That might be Barry trying to reach him. I wipe my greasy fingers on a napkin and reach for the phone.

My mouth drops open when I see the alert in the Tesla app. I click on it, my eyes widening when I see that my sister is on the move. *Game time!*

I jump to my feet, still clutching Marco's phone. I'm not going to wait for him to get out of the shower. I can't take the risk of losing Callie in case she disables mobile access in her app.

After a moment's hesitation, I snatch Marco's car keys up from the table and dart outside. There's less chance of Callie spotting me in a strange vehicle. Time to find out where my supposedly incapacitated sister is off to. If I were a gambler, I'd put money on her meeting up with Doug.

I pull out onto the street and accelerate, savoring the power of an engine that doesn't groan in protest. I'm about to send Marco a message when I remember I have his phone. He's going to be furious with me. It was reckless taking off with his phone and car like that. Our relationship has been slowly thawing out, but this might be enough to cause an Arctic freeze.

Callie is driving at a considerable speed, and I have a tough time keeping up with her on the app. I'm terrified she'll turn off access at any minute, but twenty minutes later, I've managed to position myself a few cars behind her. I lose her briefly at a junction, but catch up again, being careful to keep a few cars between us. I don't know what I'm going to do if it turns out she's meeting Doug. I'll be tempted to confront her, but the best thing to do is stay in the shadows and surveil the situation.

Once we reach the edge of town, I realize Callie is headed for the freeway. I check the gas gauge, relieved to see that Marco's tank is almost three-quarters full. If Callie's Tesla is fully charged, she could drive for several hours. I wonder if Eleanor and Theo know she's gone.

It's close to ninety minutes later before she takes the exit for Redwood Ridge. I fall back, keeping out of sight as I continue to track her on the app. She drives for a couple of miles through the suburbs and out into the countryside before finally rolling to a stop. I follow her route, and spot the Tesla sitting in the driveway of a craftsman-style bungalow in a wooded area.

I pull over and park a short distance away, then sink down in the seat to see what she'll do next. If this is where she's meeting Doug, it's a surprising choice. I'd have thought an upscale hotel or a glamorous gated Airbnb with a hot tub would have been more their style.

I watch as Callie climbs out of her Tesla, arms laden with paper bags of groceries, and makes her way up to the front door.

From my vantage spot, I film everything as discreetly as I can.

She throws a harried glance over her shoulder before letting herself in and slamming the door shut behind her.

I close my camera app and watch the bungalow for any sign of movement. If Callie and Doug are planning a weekend rendezvous, she must be expecting him any minute now.

And when he does show up, I'll be waiting. I'm not going home without the evidence I need to clear my name and put my evil sister away.

CHAPTER 76

Two hours into my stakeout, I'm beginning to think Doug's not going to show up tonight. It's already past 10:00 p.m. I'm debating giving up and heading home when my phone rings, startling me out of my reverie. An unlisted number. I ignore it and drop my phone back down on the seat. Almost immediately, Marco's phone begins to ring. I glance at it and see the same number again on the screen. I grimace. It must be Marco trying to reach. I'm tempted to brush him off, but I'm going to need to have it out with him, sooner or later.

"Hello," I say, fighting to keep my tone neutral.

"What are you playing at?" Marco growls. "What are you doing in Redwood Ridge?"

"I followed Callie here to a house on the outskirts of town. She took some groceries inside, but I have no idea if she's planning on staying here tonight. I thought she might be going to meet Doug, but he hasn't shown up yet. There aren't any other cars here except for hers, so I'm pretty sure he didn't get here ahead of her."

"I can't believe you took off without me," Marco fumes. "Do you have any idea of the danger you could be in if they spot you?"

"They won't recognize your car. Don't worry, I'm keeping a low profile."

"I am worried. You need to get out of there. They're killers, or have you forgotten that part?"

I take a couple of shallow breaths, willing myself to placate him. It's pointless arguing on the phone. "I'll give it a few more minutes and then I'll leave. Take my car if you need it."

"That's not the point. You're risking your life. Your sister's a psychopath."

"Thanks for the reminder." I end the call and toss the phone onto the seat. I have no intention of going anywhere yet. It's time to do some snooping and try to find out what Callie is up to in this neighborhood.

I clamber out of my car and make my way through the shadows toward the house. A coyote howls in the distance, making the hair on the back of my neck stand on end. When I reach the driveway, I throw a furtive glance around to make sure no one's observing me, then hurry across the lawn and slip through the wooden gate at the side of the house. I press up against the wall and take a calming breath in the cold night air. So far so good.

Tentatively, I creep around to the back of the house and hunker down beneath the kitchen window. After a few minutes, I slowly raise my head and peek inside. The room is in darkness. Has Callie gone to bed already? My frustration at the situation is mounting. Have I come all this way for nothing?

As a last resort, I try the handle on the back door. To my surprise, it's open. The patter of my heart clicks up a gear. Gingerly, I push the door inward and tiptoe inside.

I'm coming for you, Callie. You can't avoid me now.

CHAPTER 77

Blood pulses in my temples as I slowly creep across the kitchen toward the hallway. I freeze when I hear the murmur of voices coming from what I assume is the family room. Either Callie isn't alone, or she's talking to someone on the phone. I inch my way to the half-open door, silently taking a shallow breath with each step. It feels as though the reverberating drum of my beating heart is echoing around the hallway, announcing my presence. I press my back up against the wall and strain to listen in on the conversation.

"It's been too long already," a female voice says. "I'm sick of being holed up here."

"It's not safe. I'm telling you, she suspects something," Callie replies. "Have you signed that paperwork I left with you?"

"Not yet. It's on the table. Are you sure this is going to work?"

"Trust me, it will work," Callie says. "I've set up a new bank account in your name. I'll transfer the money in the morning."

I struggle to control my ragged breathing. Marco was right about Callie siphoning money into an account. But who is this woman she's talking to? Could it be Vanessa? Did she find out about the affair and demand money to keep quiet? I need to get a peek inside that room. I pad sideways a few more inches, my heart floating to the top of my throat. I peer between the door hinges, but I can't see anyone from that angle.

Gingerly, I take a step backward. My foot lands on something squishy and the squeak that follows rips through the silence in the hallway like a banshee.

"Who's there?" Callie yells.

Before I can even attempt a retreat to the kitchen, she comes flying out of the family room. Her eyes flash with anger. "You! What are you doing here?"

I fire back a defiant glare. "I could ask you the same thing. Aren't you supposed to be incapacitated, or was that all an act?"

A young woman appears in the doorway, dressed in a terry robe, pajamas, and slippers, with a towel turban twisted over her damp hair. Even without a scrap of make up on, she's drop-dead gorgeous. It takes a moment to place her, but then my heart almost stops. *No! Could it be?*

"Who is this?" she asks, her gaze swiveling from me to Callie.

"This is . . . uh, a friend of mine," Callie says. "Go to bed. I need to talk to her for a minute in private."

"What's she doing here?" the woman demands, folding her arms in front of her. "No one's supposed to—"

"I *said*, go to bed," Callie repeats through clenched teeth.

"I'm Piper Madden," I chime in. "Callie's sister."

The woman throws a nervous glance at Callie.

I take a step toward her. "Are you . . . Athena Bramston?"

Panic lights up the woman's eyes. "You're not supposed to be here."

I gasp in disbelief. "You *are* Athena! Do you have any idea how many people are looking for you? Your grandmother's beside herself. She even hired a private investigator to help find you. And I set up a missing person Facebook page."

Athena shrugs. "I don't have Wi-Fi here. And Callie took my phone." She glares at her.

"You didn't want to be found, remember?" Callie snaps.

"Athena, you need to come home with me," I say, stretching out a hand to her. "I don't know why Callie's helping you hide out here, but this is wrong."

Athena shakes her head. "I can't. My dad will go ballistic and ruin everything."

My eyes jerk to Callie. "Does she not know?"

"Know what?" Athena asks.

"You haven't told her?" I say in a hushed whisper.

Athena wrinkles her brow. "Told me what?"

Callie twists her lips. "You need to leave, Piper. You're trespassing."

I turn to Athena to plead with her one last time but freeze when the click of a gun being cocked reverberates through the shadowy hallway.

CHAPTER 78

"Callie! No!" Athena screams.

I slowly raise my hands in front of me. Marco was right. My sister is seriously deranged. I need to defuse the situation before someone gets hurt. "Put down the gun, Callie. If you want me to leave, I will."

She smirks. "I don't think so. You had your chance. I've changed my mind. Give me your purse."

Reluctantly, I slip it from my shoulder and hand it to her. There goes any hope of calling for help.

Callie gestures to the family room. "Inside, both of you."

Athena starts to cry. "I don't understand. Why are you pointing a gun at your sister? She's not going to tell anyone I'm here. Are you?"

I grimace inwardly, avoiding her eyes. I can't lie to her. I've had enough of hiding the Bramston family secrets. If I make it out of here alive, I'm going straight to the police to let them know where Athena is.

"Sit down!" Callie orders us.

Athena sinks down on the couch next to me, her robe slipping open. I gasp when I catch a glimpse of her belly. "Are you . . . pregnant?"

241

She rubs her hands affectionately over her small bump, a smile forming on her lips. "Yes."

"Is that why you ran away?"

She pulls a face. "I want to have the baby. Dad won't let me if he finds out. I've been wearing baggy clothes so no one would notice."

I shift uncomfortably at the mention of her father. As difficult as it will be for her to hear the truth, I can't let Callie deceive her any longer.

"Athena, I'm sorry to have to tell you this, but your dad—"

"What she means," Callie interrupts, pointing the gun at me, "is that she tried to convince me your dad assaulted her friend in college and that he was some kind of creep who stalked women."

Athena blinks at me in childlike bewilderment, mouth agape.

"She's lying," I say. "She told me he was stalking other women. She even showed me surveillance photos she claimed he had hidden in his closet. I believed her."

Athena covers her mouth with her hand, her chest heaving up and down. She looks like she's about to have a panic attack. I make a move toward her, but she jumps up and runs over to Callie. I grimace inwardly. I can't blame her for not believing me. Callie's the only mother figure she's ever known.

"Good girl," Callie says, patting her awkwardly on the shoulder.

"Should we call the police?" Athena asks. "We can have her arrested for trespassing."

"No. If we do that, she'll tell them you're here. I'll work something out. First, I need to restrain her. Can you keep the gun on her while I check the garage?"

"Sure." Athena takes the weapon from Callie and trains it on me.

"Just in case you think she doesn't know how to use it, you'd be wrong," Callie says. "She's been going to the gun range with her dad since she was ten years old." She leans

242

over and whispers in my ear. "Not a word about Lincoln or I'll kill you."

She strides out of the room, and I'm left staring down the barrel of the gun pointed at me by Lincoln's sixteen-year-old daughter.

"I should just shoot you now for badmouthing my dad," she says, curling her lip at me.

"I didn't. Your stepmother is a liar and a manipulator."

"Why should I believe you over her?"

"Has she ever lied to you before?"

Athena's hands tremble slightly. "Everybody lies."

I reach for the paperwork on the coffee table in front of me. "What's this document that she wants you to sign?"

"It's a bank account for me and the baby. She's helping me gain my independence."

I scan through the first few paragraphs. As I suspected, it has nothing to do with a bank account and everything to do with Callie being granted guardianship of her stepdaughter — just another way for her to get her hands on the Bramston family money.

"You don't need Callie's help," I say. "What about the father of your baby? Why don't you sue him for child support?"

A thin crease splits her forehead. "I can't do that. Dad will have him arrested."

CHAPTER 79

I chew on my lip, wanting to spare my niece the awful truth. But I can't keep her in the dark any longer. She's hiding out here from a dead man. "Athena, I . . . tried to tell you this earlier but Callie cut me off. I'm truly sorry, honey, but your father passed away a few days ago."

She gives an adamant shake of her head. "You're not going to fool me. I know what you're trying to do."

"Listen to me, Athena," I say in an urgent tone. "Your stepmother's going to be back any minute. She pushed your father down the stairs and convinced me it was an accident. I made a terrible mistake and helped her cover it up by staging a suicide. She set me up."

"No. That's a lie. It's all lies," Athena insists.

"Exactly," Callie calls out, striding back into the room with a plastic carton of zip ties. "She's nothing but a liar." She makes a beeline to me. "Put your hands behind your back."

I throw a pleading glance at Athena but she hardens her expression, keeping the gun aimed at my chest.

Reluctantly, I allow Callie to restrain me. When she's finished tightening my bonds to her satisfaction, she shoves me back down on the couch.

"She is lying, isn't she?" Athena says to her. "My dad's not really dead."

Callie lets out a heavy sigh and shakes her head at me. "You're nothing but scum — breaking my daughter's heart like that." She turns to Athena, a contrite look on her face. "I'm so sorry, darling, I was trying to protect you from it."

"She deserves to know the truth," I say. "You killed her father."

Callie lets out a scoffing laugh. "Don't let her fool you, Athena. Your aunt's about to be charged with his murder. She's out on bail. And it's not the first time she tried to kill a man either. She's been to prison before."

"She planted my DNA in your dad's Mercedes," I say. "She borrowed my hairbrush and took some hairs from it. That's why the cops arrested me."

Athena stares at me for a long moment, as though something's just clicked inside her head. She turns in Callie's direction. "You took my hairbrush a few weeks back and never returned it."

Callie raises her brows. "Really? I don't remember that. I'm sure it's here somewhere."

Athena fires her an indignant glare. "No. You left with it. I remember seeing you slip it into your purse. I didn't think much of it at the time."

I stare at Callie in horror as it dawns on me what she was planning all along. After everything that's come to light, I believe she's sick enough to try to set up Athena to take the blame for Lincoln's death. But conveniently, I came along, and she saw a better opportunity. I was a sucker for her sob story, desperate to bond with her, and dumb enough to repeat the mistakes from my past.

"You were planning on pinning Lincoln's murder on your stepdaughter before I came along, weren't you?" I ask.

"Don't be ridiculous!" Callie retorts. "You're desperate to turn Athena against me, but it won't work."

"Is that why you insisted on renting a place with no Wi-Fi?" Athena asks in a hushed tone. "So I wouldn't find out Dad was dead."

"Of course not!" Callie counters. "How could I possibly have known your aunt would kill him?"

"Don't listen to her, Athena," I say, pulling in vain against my restraints. "Take a look at the document on the coffee table. It gives Callie guardianship over you. That means she controls all the money now that your dad is dead."

Athena's lips set in a grim line. She walks over to the coffee table and picks up the paperwork, keeping the gun pointed at Callie.

"Look at the third paragraph," I say. "Callie Madden-Bramston is hereby appointed guardian of the personal estate of Athena Bramston."

The minute Athena glances down at the paperwork, Callie springs at her, tackling her to the ground.

The crack of the gun reverberates in my ears. I scream, staring in horror at the tangle of motionless bodies on the floor in front of me.

CHAPTER 80

Time screeches to a standstill as I try to grasp what just happened. At first, I think Athena and Callie are both dead, but then I detect the faintest twitch of a limb. Callie is sprawled on top of Athena, and I can't tell for sure which of them moved.

I lurch to my feet and hurry across the room, trying not to stumble. A telltale rust-colored stain is spreading through Callie's shirt. It looks like she's been shot in the stomach. I need to do something to try and stem the flow of blood, but with my hands tied behind my back, I'm pretty much helpless. I drop to my knees and lean in close. "Callie, can you hear me?"

She doesn't respond, but, beneath her body, Athena stirs, moaning softly.

"It's okay, Athena. I'm going to help you," I say, awkwardly shoving Callie off her with my body.

She groans again, her eyes fluttering open.

"Athena! It's me, Piper," I say, leaning over her.

She blinks up at me, as if trying to remember who I am, or where she might have seen me before.

"Are you hurt?" I ask.

She rolls slowly onto her side, clutching her belly. "I don't think so. But I don't know about the baby. What happened?"

247

My gaze travels slowly over her. She looks genuinely confused. Does she not remember? She must have been knocked out in the scuffle for the gun.

"Callie tackled you and the gun went off," I say. I don't know if it really was an accident, or if Athena deliberately shot her, but I know the version of events we're going to need to stick with. "Where is the gun?"

"It must be underneath her." Athena groans as she grabs onto a nearby chair and struggles to her feet.

She glances tentatively at Callie. "Is she . . . dead?"

I grimace. "I think so. Can you check for a pulse?"

She shivers. "I don't want to touch her."

"Fine. I'll do it as soon as you fetch some scissors or a knife to cut me free."

She disappears out the door, and I scoot closer to Callie, trying to detect any sign of breathing. I can't believe she's dead. I feel numb at the thought — unsure if I should be broken over losing her, or relieved, or indifferent, or some combination of emotions.

Athena returns with a pair of scissors and snips the zip ties off my wrists. I immediately place my index and middle fingers on Callie's neck. My heart jolts halfway up my throat when I detect a faint pulse. "She's alive!" I gasp. I pull Callie's phone from her pocket and toss it to Athena. "Call 911." I yank my sweatshirt over my head and press it to Callie's stomach.

Athena stares down at the phone in her hands as though it's a grenade.

"Athena!" I yell. "Are you listening to me?"

"I'm going to prison, aren't I?" she answers, her voice quavering. "If she survives, she'll say I tried to kill her."

"No!" I grab her by the wrist. "You need to trust me. It was self-defense."

"But—"

"We don't have time for this, Athena. Call for help, now! I'm going to start CPR."

She gives a reluctant nod. "I can't stay here and watch," she says, retreating out of the room.

I focus all my efforts on trying to remember everything I learned in the CPR class I took years ago, but my brain is stalling. I can't recall how many compressions I'm supposed to do, or how fast I should be doing them. And what do I do if Callie stops breathing before the ambulance gets here? Tentatively, I slide my hand beneath her body and feel around for the gun, but I can't reach it.

Panic swells inside me when I see how quickly my sweatshirt is filling with blood. At this rate, Callie will bleed out before the emergency services get here. "Athena?" I call over my shoulder. "Athena, are you there?"

I'm about to get to my feet to go look for her when a strange gurgling sound comes from Callie's lips.

CHAPTER 81

"Callie!" I scream, as though my desperate cry might somehow reverse course on her dying breaths. I drop back down at her side and push down on her chest. I count out loud, frantically trying to remember when I need to give a rescue breath.

"Athena! I need you!" I yell at the top of my lungs.

I pinch Callie's nose and blow a couple of breaths into her mouth, but her chest doesn't move. I repeat the process, sweating profusely from sheer panic. Am I doing it right? Where on earth is Athena? I hope nothing's wrong with the baby. And why is it taking so long for an ambulance to get here?

I don't know how long I keep at the chest compressions until I collapse on my sister's body and admit defeat. After a moment or two, I fall back on my haunches and stare at my blood-soaked hands before staggering to my feet.

I dash into the hallway and call up the stairs. "Athena! Are you all right?" I listen for a response but get nothing. Fear thrums through me when I remember she was clutching her stomach. What if she has miscarried and is passed out somewhere? I jump to my feet and jog up the stairs, peering into every room. There's no sign of her anywhere. I tear back down the stairs and run to the kitchen. Relief floods through me when I spot her on the phone just outside the back door.

I yank it all the way open. "Is the ambulance on its way?"

She puts a finger to her lips and nods.

I go back inside the house and pour myself a glass of water. My hands are shaking so badly I lean over the sink to drink it but still manage to spill half of it in the process. I retreat to the family room and perch on the arm of the couch, staring numbly at my sister's body.

A few minutes later, Athena walks back inside.

"I couldn't revive her," I say.

"I'm glad," Athena responds. "She didn't deserve to live after what she did."

I spin around and stare at her in horror. "Don't say that. She was still your stepmother."

"She was nothing but a freeloader." She gestures to the paperwork still lying on the coffee table. "You were right. She wasn't looking out for me and the baby. She wanted my dad's money for herself."

I set my lips in a grim line. "She was embezzling money from some of your dad's accounts. I don't know how much of that was her idea, but I think she had help with it. I'm pretty sure she was having an affair with her next-door neighbor."

Athena's head swivels in my direction, her eyes bulging. "What?"

"Doug Ridley was helping her commit financial fraud. I'm not sure what else they were planning, but I think it involved doing away with both you and your dad so they could get their hands on his money."

Athena pales. "You're lying! Doug would never help Callie steal dad's money."

"I know it's hard to believe, and I wish it wasn't true, but I saw an email on Callie's computer from him. He was asking if she'd said anything to Lincoln. He ended it by saying: *You know our love is real.*"

Athena's expression relaxes. She rubs a hand affectionately over her belly. "You've got it all wrong. He wasn't talking about his love for Callie."

251

CHAPTER 82

My skin crawls as the truth hits me like a linebacker, knocking the breath from my lungs and splintering my brain. Doug didn't seduce his next-door neighbor's wife — he seduced his next-door neighbor's underage daughter. Callie must have found out about the affair and threatened to tell Lincoln. Was she blackmailing Doug into helping her siphon money from Lincoln's bank accounts in return for her silence? A man in Doug's position might be willing to do anything to avoid the threat of prison — including murder.

"What's wrong? Lost for words all of a sudden?" Athena giggles.

"This isn't funny," I say. "Callie killed your dad, and she was planning on framing you for the murder until I came along — why else would she have taken your hairbrush, if not for insurance? You're in danger."

"Not anymore. She's dead. I'm safe now."

"No, you're not. Doug was in on it. He helped Callie with the financial fraud, and I suspect he helped her get rid of your dad too."

"You don't know Doug like I do," Athena says. "He loves me. He wouldn't do anything to hurt me. We're going to get married once I turn eighteen."

"He's fooling you. Think about it. He can't let you have that baby. If he does, he'll go to prison."

"Not if no one knows he's the father."

"Callie knew. She might have told someone else. And I know now."

Athena narrows her eyes at me. Slowly, she slips her hand into the pocket of her robe and pulls out the gun.

I back up a step or two, blood roaring in my ears. I can't believe she had the wherewithal to hide it from me. "Athena, put down the gun. You don't know what you're doing."

"Don't I? Ask Callie if she agrees with that."

My heart sinks. So, it wasn't an accident, after all. "Why aren't the emergency services here yet?" I ask.

"I didn't call them."

The nape of my neck prickles. "Who were you talking to on the phone?"

"Someone who cares about me."

I frown. "Your grandmother?"

Athena scowls. "Not likely."

I open my mouth to respond but freeze when I spot headlights in the driveway.

CHAPTER 83

My heart knocks against my ribs. Could that be the police? Did someone hear the gunshot and call it in? I dash to the front door and strain to see through the glass. No flashing lights. What if it's a neighbor? How on earth are we going to explain a pregnant teenager with a gun, and a dead body lying on the floor?

"Get away from the door," Athena hisses, waving the gun at me.

"Okay, take it easy!" I say, retreating a few steps.

She walks up to the door and reaches out to unlatch it.

"Wait! Put the gun away first," I cry. "We don't know who's out there."

She glares defiantly at me as she yanks the door open.

I gasp at the sight of a stone-faced Doug Ridley standing on the steps. This must be who Athena was talking to on the phone. She doesn't realize the danger she's put us both in. I need to get a hold of that gun before he does.

He slams the door shut behind him, and Athena immediately throws herself at him. "I've missed you so much!"

"Where is she?" he asks, extricating himself from her embrace.

"In the family room."

"We'll take care of this sister first," Doug says, grabbing me by the arm.

"There are zip ties on the couch," Athena says.

"You'll never get away with this," I say, struggling to free myself from Doug's iron grasp. "Eleanor Bramston will make sure you go to prison for the rest of your life when she finds out what you've done to her granddaughter."

Doug moves his jaw side to side, a grim cast to his face. "Then we'll just have to make sure she never finds out, won't we?"

I thrash around trying to break free, but he punches me on the side of the head, leaving me dazed enough for him to secure my hands behind my back and throw me down on the couch.

My chest heaves up and down as he walks over to my sister's body and surveys the damage in a clinical manner. "It's too much blood. We'll have to roll her up in the rug and toss everything," he says to Athena.

"Where are you going to take her?" she asks in a hushed tone.

"Leave that up to me. The less you know the better." He takes off his jacket and rolls up his sleeves.

Athena sets the gun down on the end table next to her.

"You'll need to wipe your prints off that," Doug says. He shoots me a scathing look. "When they find the body, the only prints on the gun will be her sister's — the same sister who's facing charges in Lincoln's murder. Should be an open-and-shut case."

He turns to Athena, his lips stretching into a salesman's smile. "Especially if you testify, my darling. She's going to prison anyway, so she might as well take the hit."

Athena throws me an uncertain look.

"Go clean off the gun and put on some gloves," Doug tells her.

She nods and hurries out of the room, leaving me alone with him.

"You're going to get rid of her too, aren't you?" I say. "That poor girl believes every lie you're spoon-feeding her."

Doug shoots me a vicious smile. "You think you're just as clever as your sister, don't you? She tried to outsmart me and look how she ended up."

"Athena's only a child."

Doug lets out a scoffing laugh. "Does she look like a child to you? Believe me, she's all woman. As manipulative as the best of them."

"You're a sick man. You killed Lincoln, didn't you? You were forced to do whatever Callie told you to do because of the terrible secret you were hiding."

He leers at me. "And now I'm free. Or about to be."

Silent as a cat, Athena glides back into the room. She raises the gun and points it at Doug.

CHAPTER 84

"Athena, sweetheart, what are you doing? Put down the gun," Doug wheedles.

"Did you kill my father?" Athena rasps.

"No! Of course not! Whatever she's told you, it's a lie. Your stepmother killed your father for his money, and she was planning on killing you too. I've been desperate to find you, but she kept insisting that you ran away, and she didn't know where you were."

"How do you know she was planning to kill me?"

Doug stretches out his hands in a placating gesture. "Look what she did to you. She whisked you away in the middle of the night and kept you holed up here. No one knew where you were. And then she lured her sister here. She'd already managed to pin Lincoln's murder on her, why not yours too?"

"That's not true," I cut in. "Callie had no idea I was coming here. I hacked into her Tesla app and followed her."

Athena eyes me curiously. "Why did you follow her?"

I lock eyes with her, willing her to believe me. "I knew she was hiding something. I thought she had planned a rendezvous with Doug. I never imagined she would lead me to you."

"Athena, give me the gun," Doug coaxes. "Think of the stress this is putting on our baby."

The determination in Athena's expression falters, and the gun begins to shake in her hand. I tense as the world moves in slow motion before my eyes. I don't have time to warn her before Doug lunges for her. At the last second, a bolt of adrenaline goes through me, and I stick out my leg and trip him, sending him flying and landing at her feet. I watch in disbelief as Athena raises the gun and pistol whips him on the back of the head. He lets out a grunt and collapses, lying motionless only a few feet from Callie's body.

Athena drops to her knees next to him, sobbing. The gun slips from her hands, and this time I don't let it out of my sight. If Doug comes around and gets a hold of it, Athena and I are both dead.

"Cut me free," I say, darting over to her. "Hurry!"

She eyes me dubiously. "But—"

"I promise you everything's going to be all right. I'm your witness to everything that happened here. It was a clear-cut case of self-defense. Your grandmother will get you a good lawyer, and you and your baby will both be safe from the tyrannical adults who took advantage of you."

To my relief, Athena complies and cuts me free once more. I reach for the gun, then grab some of the leftover zip ties and secure Doug's hands behind his back. It feels good to return the favor.

"What's going to happen to him?" Athena asks.

I release a tired breath. Now's not the time to shatter her dreams. "That's not for us to decide. All we need to worry about is doing the right thing. It's time to make the call you should have made the first time."

CHAPTER 85

Six Weeks Later

I can't believe Marco and I are standing on Eleanor and Theo Bramston's front steps again — this time as invited guests to what I suspect will be the baby shower of the year, even for this ritzy neighborhood. Based on what Athena has told me, her grandmother has gone out of her way to cater to her every wish, even going so far as to hire an expensive event planning company that promises "an unforgettable experience." Contrary to Athena's fears, Eleanor is wholly embracing the impending birth of another Bramston male. I suspect this baby will go a long way to helping the family heal.

A uniformed maid ushers us into the great room, where a harpist is playing softly in an alcove beneath a crystal chandelier.

"Piper! Marco! So glad you two could make it," Eleanor gushes.

A server dressed in black appears out of nowhere balancing a tray filled with champagne flutes. Marco and I politely decline. "Just some water when you get a chance, thanks," I say.

"Help yourselves to hors d'oeuvres," Eleanor says, drifting off to mingle with the other guests. I let out a silent sigh of relief. I still feel guilty every time I'm in her presence. To this day, she has no idea that I helped dispose of her son's body, and she never will. Thanks to attorney–client privilege, Barry never disclosed my participation in Callie's crime.

I glance around the room, searching for Athena. I can't help but be awed by the opulent decor and luxurious setting we're standing in. This baby will want for nothing if this is how he's celebrated before he even arrives.

White helium balloons, arranged like clouds, hover over us in the eighteen-foot ceiling space. Blue and white flowers in cascading arrangements are dotted throughout the room, interspersed by round tables draped in blue silk linens and set with fine china. An elaborate five-tiered cake that could rival any wedding cake sits front and center at the dessert station. I make a mental note to take a picture to show Jenna later.

The server returns with two cut-crystal tumblers full of ice water. Gingerly, I reach for a glass, hoping I don't break it. It's probably worth more than the entire contents of my apartment.

I take a tentative sip of water just as Athena waltzes into the room looking radiant in a blue satin dress. Her face lights up when she sees me.

"Piper!" She runs over and embraces me, and I clutch her tightly in return. We may not be related by blood, but for better or worse, we're bonded through the bad blood that brought us together.

"You look so glamorous," I say, holding her out at arm's length to admire her. "How are you feeling?"

"Excited." Her smile falters. "It's been hard. I wasn't planning on doing this without him."

She doesn't need to spell it out. She's had to come to terms with the fact that the father of her baby will be behind bars for the best years of his child's life. And if Eleanor Bramston has her way, he won't be allowed anywhere near her grandchild once he's released either.

On a brighter note, Athena's claim of self-defense in Callie's death wasn't challenged, and the obstruction charges against me were dropped shortly afterward. The police managed to trace the anonymous messages I received back to a teenage tech whiz Callie had hired, which bolstered my defense that she tried to frame me. As far as the rest of the world knows, she was the female driver who almost rammed into the back of a truck the night Lincoln died. I guess a person can only steal so many hairbrushes before it becomes apparent they were planting evidence.

"You're going to be a wonderful mother," I assure Athena. "And you have doting grandparents to support you."

She takes my hands in hers. "Thank you for everything." She glances over at Marco, who's deep in conversation with Theo. "And please thank Marco again for all his help. If it hadn't been for him and his tech wizardry, you would never have found me."

I nod. "He's a good guy."

Eleanor claps her hands to get everyone's attention, then proposes a toast to Athena and her unborn son, Louis Michael Bramston. It's the first time I've heard his name. It sounds impressive, like he's really going to be someone — hopefully nothing like the other male figures in his bloodline.

After the ceremonial present opening, accompanied by the requisite *oohs* and *aahs*, Marco and I make a quiet exit.

"That was quite the do," I say, when we pull up outside his house a short time later.

"Not sure how to describe it," he replies. "Excessive doesn't cut it."

"They must have had thousands of dollars in balloon clouds alone."

He laughs. "Too flashy for me. I'm a simple man."

"It doesn't take much to make me happy either," I say. "Just the smell of freshly baked flaky pastry in the morning."

"You know what would make me happy?" Marco says, reaching over and taking my hand. "Spending the rest of my life with you."

261

EPILOGUE

Two Years Later

> *Dear Callie,*
>
> I promised myself I would write you a letter every year
> on your birthday as a way to remember you and the relation-
> ship we might have had if things had worked out differently.
> Not that you'll ever read this. Truthfully, writing out my
> thoughts is cathartic for me as I try to heal from the scars you
> seared on my soul.
>
> It's been another eventful year. I wish you could have
> been here to experience it with me. I penned a bestseller! Bet
> you didn't think I had it in me. I never in a million years
> anticipated it becoming such a hit, but it blew up overnight.
> It's even been optioned for movie rights. Can you believe it?
> I'm still pinching myself. I purchased my first new car a few
> days ago with my earnings, and I can actually afford to put
> gas in it. Even better, I bought the Wicked Scone, and Jenna
> was finally able to retire.
>
> You incinerated my heart when you accused me of only
> being after your money. I confess I was more than a little

envious of your lifestyle — maybe we had more in common that I wanted to admit — but I never asked for a handout, and I never took what wasn't mine. So, it's kind of ironic that, in the end, I made a boatload of money off you.

I don't consider myself a parasite — I didn't make my wealth at your expense. I like to think of myself as more of a vulture, feasting on the carrion you left behind in your crime spree of fraud, deception, and murder. Yes, you guessed it, I co-opted our story, with some heavy editing in parts. I wasn't going to incriminate myself, but I couldn't let it all be for nothing — not after everything I risked for you.

I've been doing the interview circuit on multiple news networks, and I'm getting hundreds of emails and letters from people who've been impacted by our story or can relate in some way or another to my struggle to get past what happened to Emma. I feel like I've found my calling at last — helping others overcome the negative emotions anchoring them to their pasts. You can run on anger a long time, but the fumes are poisonous.

What else is new? Vanessa divorced Doug — no surprise there — and moved back to her hometown in New York. Rumor has it she's dating some big-shot hedge fund manager now.

Louis, Athena's little boy, is walking and talking. He's a beautiful child who, sadly, or perhaps fortuitously, will never know his father. Doug Ridley took his own life before he went to trial — the coward couldn't face the thought of doing prison time for what he'd done. Athena was in shock and depressed for months afterward, but she's since moved on and is focused on finishing school, with the help of her grandparents, who dote on Louis.

I've saved the biggest news of all for last. Marco and I tied the knot three weeks ago at a lowkey courthouse wedding witnessed by Jenna. I can't tell you how happy I am to be married to my best friend. I always knew he would do anything

263

for me, just like I would have done anything for you. Loving someone is a gamble, but if you never throw your heart in the ring, you'll never know what it is to be touched by humanity's greatest force. Too bad you never gave us a shot.

Until next year,
Your sister, Piper

THE END

THE JOFFE BOOKS STORY

We began in 2014 when Jasper agreed to publish his mum's much-rejected romance novel and it became a bestseller.

Since then we've grown into the largest independent publisher in the UK. We're extremely proud to publish some of the very best writers in the world, including Joy Ellis, Faith Martin, Caro Ramsay, Helen Forrester, Simon Brett and Robert Goddard. Everyone at Joffe Books loves reading and we never forget that it all begins with the magic of an author telling a story.

We are proud to publish talented first-time authors, as well as established writers whose books we love introducing to a new generation of readers.

We won Trade Publisher of the Year at the Independent Publishing Awards in 2023 and Best Publisher Award in 2024 at the People's Book Prize. We have been shortlisted for Independent Publisher of the Year at the British Book Awards for the last five years, and were shortlisted for the Diversity and Inclusivity Award at the 2022 Independent Publishing Awards. In 2023 we were shortlisted for Publisher of the Year at the RNA Industry Awards, and in 2024 we were shortlisted at the CWA Daggers for the Best Crime and Mystery Publisher.

We built this company with your help, and we love to hear from you, so please email us about absolutely anything bookish at feedback@joffebooks.com.

If you want to receive free books every Friday and hear about all our new releases, join our mailing list here: www.joffebooks.com/freebooks.

And when you tell your friends about us, just remember: it's pronounced Joffe as in coffee or toffee!